Now, he thoug...

Now's the time, now... ... could he say? How could he convince her that he loved her when he was never going to be able to make the kind of flattering speeches that tripped so easily off Mark's tongue?

Show her, his heart suggested. Show her you care, that the love is still there.

'Helen...' He cleared his throat, and started again. 'Will you come to bed with me?'

Was it his imagination or had her grip on the magazine tightened?

'Helen, please.' Dear Lord, he was begging. 'Helen, it's been so long since we made love, and...and I need you.' Slowly she lowered the magazine, and to his utter horror he could see tears sparkling in her eyes. Oh, hell, could he never get it right? 'Helen, I'm sorry. Oh, love, don't—please, don't cry.'

Desperately he reached for her, and she met him halfway, clinging to him with an almost frantic need.

'Kiss me, Tom,' she muttered into his ... 'Don't talk—don't say anything. Just...kiss me.'

THE BABY DOCTORS

The gynaecology department at the Belfield Infirmary,
Glasgow, is a very special place, and it employs a very
special team of people. Doctors who are all dedicated
to helping patients fulfil their dreams for a family by
helping them bring babies safely into the world.
Some of these doctors have families of their own;
some are still searching. Some of them are married
to each other; some of them are meant for each other.
But, whatever their personal problems,
they are all committed to giving their patients
the best chance of a child.

**For THE BABY DOCTORS—
making families is their business.**

Look out for the next book in this emotional trilogy
from Maggie Kingsley, where you can find out if the
charms of outsider David Hart work on the spiky
Special Registrar Rachel Dunwoody.

Medical Romance™…medical drama on the pulse

THE SURGEON'S MARRIAGE

BY

MAGGIE KINGSLEY

MILLS & BOON®

All the characters in this book have no existence outside the imagination of the author, and have no relation whatsoever to anyone bearing the same name or names. They are not even distantly inspired by any individual known or unknown to the author, and all the incidents are pure invention.

First published in Great Britain 2003
Harlequin Mills & Boon Limited,
Eton House, 18-24 Paradise Road, Richmond, Surrey TW9 1SR

© Maggie Kingsley 2003

ISBN 0 263 83437 9

Set in Times Roman 10½ on 11¼ pt.
03-0403-51075

Printed and bound in Spain
by Litografía Rosés, S.A., Barcelona

CHAPTER ONE

HELEN stared at the damp towel hanging over the banister. It was strange how something so ordinary, so innocuous, could set your teeth on edge. Especially when it was nothing new. In fact, every morning for the past ten years Tom had come out of the shower and thrown his towel over that self-same banister.

Then why don't you simply tell him to stop doing it? her mind asked as she lifted the towel and carried it down the stairs to the kitchen. Tell him it's driving you crazy.

'Because if I do,' she told the potted plant on the window-sill, 'Tom will say, "If it bothers you that much, why didn't you mention it before?"'

And she'd be forced to admit that it hadn't bothered her before, but now it did, and Tom would either frown uncomprehendingly or smile in that horribly knowing fashion which meant, Oops, it must be Helen's time of the month again so I'd better tread carefully.

Tears filled her eyes, and she angrily blinked them away. It wasn't her time of the month. She wished it was. At least then she'd have some excuse for the odd feelings of dissatisfaction and irritation which had been plaguing her recently. And she had nothing to be dissatisfied about. She had a good marriage, two healthy, beautiful children, a job she loved—

'Mum, I can't find my white T-shirt, and I need it for gymnastics.'

She glanced round to see her daughter standing in the kitchen doorway. 'If you need it for gymnastics you should have told me yesterday.'

'But I *always* have gymnastics on Mondays—you know I do. Tuesday's art, Wednesday's—'

'Your green one's washed and ironed.'

'But everyone else will be wearing white. I'll be the odd one out—'

'Mum, have you seen my trainers?'

'*I'm* talking to Mum,' Emma protested.

'Big deal,' her brother exclaimed. 'Mum, my trainers…'

'They're in your wardrobe, John. Which is where you should have put them when you got home from school on Friday, instead of just dumping them down in the hall,' Helen called after her son as he dashed away.

'Mum, about my white T-shirt. Couldn't you—?'

'Helen, it's half past eight. Are you ready to go?'

'Does it look like I am?' she protested, seeing her husband's head come round the kitchen door. 'Emma, I'm sorry, but you're going to have to wear your green T-shirt, and that's final.'

Emma wandered unhappily away, and Tom's eyebrows rose. 'Problems?'

'Just the usual Monday morning mayhem,' Helen said irritably, taking a scrunchy out of her pocket and twisting her shoulder-length blonde hair back into a ponytail. 'Honestly, there are times when I wonder why we ever had children.'

'Because of one split condom nine years ago?' Tom grinned, and a reluctant smile curved her own lips.

That faulty condom had a lot to answer for. For a start it had put paid to their plans when they'd got married not to have children until they were both Obs and Gynae specialist registrars. Tom had made the grade, but it had never been an option for her, not after the twins had been born.

She'd never regretted it. OK, so perhaps occasionally she thought it would have been nice if both she and Tom could have fulfilled their dreams, but the children were a joy and a delight when they weren't driving her mad, and being an Obs and Gynae SHO was responsibility enough when you had a pair of lively eight-year-olds to look after.

'That's the school bus,' Tom declared as a horn sounded outside. He glanced down at his watch and frowned. 'Helen, I hate to hurry you, but we really do have to go. I'll start the car, shall I?'

The smile on her lips died. He couldn't perhaps have offered to wash the breakfast dishes first, or tidy up the sitting room? No, of course he couldn't. The dishes would still be waiting for her when she got home tonight, and the sitting room would still look as though a bomb had hit it.

Oh, stop it, Helen, she told herself as she shepherded Emma and John out to the school bus, trying hard to ignore Emma's reproachful expression which said all too clearly, Everyone else's mum would have remembered my T-shirt. Tom's a good husband, a loving husband, and you know he would have washed the dishes in a minute if you'd asked him. Yes, but I shouldn't *need* to ask him, she argued back. He should have *known*.

'Everything OK, love?' Tom asked, shooting her a puzzled frown as she got into the car beside him, then fastened her seat belt.

'Fine,' she managed to reply, but everything wasn't fine. Not by a long shot.

Tom would probably have said she was simply suffering from a bad case of overwork, and maybe she was. This last month at the Belfield Infirmary had certainly been a nightmare, what with Rachel Dunwoody suddenly taking compassionate leave because of the death of her aunt, then Annie Hart and Gideon Caldwell getting married.

Not that she begrudged the junior doctor and ward consultant their happiness—in fact, she'd been delighted when they'd finally got together—and poor Rachel had obviously been shattered by her aunt's death so it wasn't surprising she'd asked for time off, but all the upheaval had meant so much extra work for her and Tom, and she was feeling it.

'This friend of yours who's standing in for Rachel,' she said as Tom negotiated the busy rush-hour traffic. 'You said he's been working in Australia for the last ten years?'

Tom nodded. 'Mark headed out to Sydney right after he qualified. He worked there for a couple of years, then moved to a senior house officer's post in Canberra, and he's been working as a specialist registrar for the last eighteen months in Melbourne.'

'And he's going to Canada in six weeks,' she said, trying and failing to keep the envy out of her voice. She'd wanted to work abroad, too, when she'd been younger, but then the children had arrived, and the years had flown by, and here she was still living and working in Glasgow. 'I hope he isn't going to find us too boring after all his travelling.'

'Why should he think we're boring?' Tom said in surprise. 'I don't think we're boring and, knowing Mark, he's probably only going to Canada because some irate boyfriend is after him.'

'Some irate boyfriend?' she repeated, bewildered, and her husband grinned.

'Back in med school there wasn't a girl who wasn't potty about him. In fact, he actually had the nerve to poach a couple of my girlfriends, but…' He shook his head ruefully. 'The crazy thing is we still stayed friends. Maybe it's because he could always make me see the funny side of things.'

'Charming as well as handsome,' she observed. 'Sounds like a pretty potent combination.'

'It is. Mind you, I'm talking about the Mark Lorimer I knew a long time ago. Ten years of Australian sun, sea and food could have made him fat, bald and charmless.'

'Is that true concern I hear, Tom Brooke, or a bad case

of wishful thinking?' she teased, and her husband's lips quirked.

'What do you think?'

That he had no need to envy his friend, she decided. Tom was a good-looking man—better-looking now, in fact, than he'd been when they'd first met. At twenty-four he'd been a lanky six-footer, with a shock of brown hair, and a pair of smiling grey eyes. Ten years on, the hair and eyes were still the same, but he'd filled out, grown more muscular, and it suited him.

I've filled out a bit in the last ten years, too, she thought wryly, but I doubt if anyone would say it suited me.

She was snacking too much, that was the trouble, but she never seemed to have time for a proper meal. If she wasn't racing round Obs and Gynae, she was chasing after John and Emma, making sure they'd done their homework properly and had clean clothes to wear for the next day.

Apart from white T-shirts, she thought guiltily, suddenly remembering Emma's disgruntled face. She'd wash and iron it tonight, after she'd done the weekly shop at the supermarket.

'Helen, are you quite sure you're OK?'

She looked up blankly to see they'd arrived at the Belfield Infirmary and Tom was gazing at her with concern.

'Of course I am,' she replied, bewildered. 'Why shouldn't I be?'

'Because...' To her surprise he suddenly reached out and gently cupped her cheek in his hand. 'I've been speaking to you for the last five minutes, and I swear you haven't heard a word.'

To her acute dismay the tears she'd felt earlier began to resurface, and she gulped them down quickly.

'I'm fine—honestly I am,' she replied with a shaky smile. 'Just...just a little tired.'

He swore under his breath. 'It's all the extra hours

you've been working recently, not to mention having to look after John and Emma and me. Look, why don't I do the weekly shop tonight—give you a break?'

For a second she was tempted, then a bubble of laughter came from her. 'Tom, if you do the shopping I know exactly what will happen. You'll come back from the supermarket with enough food to feed an army, plus a whole load of stuff that nobody likes because you noticed it was on special offer.'

His lips curved. 'What if I promise to stick to your list?'

'*I'll* do the shopping. I'm OK—really I am,' she insisted, seeing his frown reappear. 'Now that Mark Lorimer's starting work today, everything will be fine.'

And it would be, she told herself as she got out of the car and followed Tom into the hospital. With the department fully staffed again she wouldn't be so tired all the time, and stupid, niggling little things wouldn't keep irritating her. She knew they wouldn't.

'OK, cheer me up on a cold April day,' she instructed Annie when she found the junior doctor in the staffroom, getting ready to go off duty. 'Tell me the ward was quiet last night, that not one single emergency came in, then give me permission to go home.'

'You don't want cheering up,' Annie protested. 'You want a miracle.'

'I know, but it was worth a try.' Helen laughed. 'OK, what's the current situation?'

'Mrs Foster burst some of her stitches last night. Apparently she was straining to pass a motion— Yes, I know,' the junior doctor said as Helen groaned. 'Not the brightest thing in the world to do when you've just had a hysterectomy, but there you go. Mrs Dawn accidentally dislodged her catheter at midnight—'

'Oh, no.'

'And—*and*,' Annie continued, 'just to add to the overall

fun and excitement, Mrs Alexander suddenly developed a deep-vein thrombosis in her leg.'

'Is she all right?' Helen asked with concern.

'Gideon's put her on anticoagulants, and we've got her in compression stockings, but it looks like we could be in for big problems when she gives birth.'

It did. Mary Alexander was thirty-six weeks pregnant, and she'd only been sent in by her GP because he thought her blood pressure was a little high. A Caesarean might be the answer, but if the clot moved to her lungs during the operation…

'I'll have a word with her once I've done the ward round,' Helen murmured, and Annie grimaced.

'A word is probably all you'll have time for. Honestly, Helen, I feel like I'm living at the hospital at the moment, and if Gideon hadn't insisted on me employing a home help I don't know how I would have managed with Jamie.'

Helen nodded. She could remember only too well how hard it had been when her own children were smaller, trying to juggle their needs and the demands of her job, and it was doubly difficult for Annie. Gideon wasn't Jamie's father, and although the little boy obviously liked the consultant, it would take time for him to accept his mother's new husband completely.

'Things will be better now Dr Lorimer's here,' she said encouragingly as she followed Annie out of the staffroom. 'With the department fully staffed again—'

'But he's not here. At least, not unless he's hiding in a cupboard.'

Helen came to a halt. 'What do you mean, he's not here? He phoned Tom from London last night to say he was just about to board the Glasgow plane.'

And to reminisce about old times, she thought, remembering the gales of laughter she'd heard coming from her husband when he'd taken the call.

'Maybe he's got lost between the airport and the

Belfield. Maybe he's taken one look at what passes for
spring weather in Britain, and headed straight back to
sunny Australia. All I know is—' Annie bit off the rest of
what she'd been about to say, and groaned. 'Oh, Lord.
Why do I know this means trouble?'

Helen turned in the direction of the junior doctor's gaze,
and her heart sank, too. Gideon was striding towards them,
looking tight-lipped and harassed, and Tom didn't look
any happier beside him.

'I'm afraid we've got a problem,' the consultant declared without preamble. 'Dr Lorimer's still in London.
Apparently Heathrow Airport's fogbound, and though he's
hoping to make it to the Belfield by mid-afternoon, we're
not to hold our breaths.'

'And?' Helen asked with foreboding, sensing there was
a very definite 'and' hanging in the air, and equally certain
she wasn't going to like it.

'We've got a postpartum haemorrhage on our hands. I'm
on my way to it now. Tom's going to take my morning
clinic, but that means—'

'You want me to take Tom's,' Helen finished for him
unhappily.

'Sorry, Helen.'

So was she. She hated taking somebody else's clinic at
short notice. It meant seeing people 'blind', with scarcely
enough time to read through their notes, but it couldn't be
helped. Emergencies were just that. Unexpected events that
nobody could predict.

'Look, would it help if I stayed on for a couple of
hours?' Annie said, beginning to unbutton her coat. 'Jamie
will be at the day-care centre by now—'

'What I want is for you to go home and get some sleep,'
Gideon said firmly. 'You've just finished a full night shift.'

'Yes, but if we're short-staffed—'

'Home, Annie. Now.'

'Three weeks married, and already he's bossing me

about,' the junior doctor protested, and Helen laughed, only for her laughter to die when Gideon suddenly put his arm around his wife and kissed her.

It wasn't a passionate kiss—the ward corridor was hardly the place for it—but as the couple drew apart a hard lump formed in her throat.

When was the last time Tom had looked at her the way Gideon was looking at Annie? When was the last time she'd looked at Tom with such obvious love in her eyes?

Good grief, woman, you've been married for ten years, not three weeks, a little voice protested at the back of her mind. You can't expect either you and Tom to be still wandering round in that heady, crazy state of euphoria that couples feel when they first fall in love.

No, her heart whispered, but surely I should be able to remember when he last told me he loved me. Surely I should at least be able to remember when we last made love.

Her heart contracted and, unable to bear looking at the couple any longer, she began walking down the corridor, only to discover Tom had come after her.

'I'm sorry,' she said, coming to an awkward halt. 'Did you want to talk to me about your clinic?'

'What I'm more interested in—more worried about—is you,' her husband replied. 'Helen, what is it—what's wrong?'

He looked anxious and perplexed, but as she stared up at him she also saw that he looked completely exhausted, and a wave of guilt surged through her. He'd been working so hard at the hospital recently—much harder than she had been—and yet here she was, feeling sorry for herself just because they hadn't made love in ages. And it was as much her fault as his. 'I'm too tired, Tom' had become her stock reply to any overture he might have made recently.

'Nothing's wrong,' she said swiftly. 'I'm just thinking about your poor friend, stuck in London—'

'But you looked so pale just a minute ago,' he pressed. 'Quite white, in fact.'

'That'll teach me to forget to put on any make-up.' She smiled, trying to lighten his mood, but it didn't work.

'You don't hear me when I'm talking to you,' he continued. 'You're tired all the time, and now your colour's coming and going. Look, perhaps you should let me examine you, give you a thorough check-up.'

'You just want an excuse to get my clothes off,' she said, her brown eyes dancing, 'and you don't need one. We're married, remember?'

'Helen, be serious.'

'Life's too short,' she insisted. 'Tom, I've been thinking—why don't we hire a babysitter the next time we both have a weekend off? We could head off somewhere romantic like the Isle of Skye. We haven't been anywhere alone for ages, and—'

'Do you think you could be hitting an early menopause?'

Her jaw dropped. 'Do I *what?*'

'I know you're only thirty-two,' he continued thoughtfully, 'but it would certainly explain your mood swings, your abstraction and fatigue—'

'Tom, I am *not* starting the menopause,' she snapped. 'If I look tired, maybe it's because I *am* tired. Tired of cooking and cleaning. Tired of constantly tidying up after you and the kids, and tired of being expected to be a superefficient SHO into the bargain.'

The words were out of her mouth before she could stop them, and she bit her lip. She hadn't realised she'd been feeling so put upon and taken for granted lately, but now she'd said it she knew it was true. It might have been better, though, if she'd couched her complaint in less confrontational language. Her husband clearly thought so, judging by the dull flush of colour sweeping across his face.

'Tom—'

'Sorry to interrupt you, Doctors,' the department secretary declared, 'but it's twenty past nine, and your clinics were supposed to start at nine.'

'Our clinics will start when we're ready to start,' Tom replied, his voice uncharacteristically brusque. 'Until then I'd be obliged if you'd allow us some privacy.'

Doris looked crushed. She also looked curious. Very curious.

'That wasn't the smartest thing in the world to do,' Helen protested the minute the woman had gone. 'Doris is the biggest gossip in the hospital, and just because you're angry with me—'

'I don't think this is the time or the place for a discussion about our private life, do you?' he said stiffly.

Oh, really? she thought. Well, she wasn't the one who'd started it with all this stupid talk about the menopause. She wasn't the one who hadn't been pulling her weight at home.

'Fine,' she said, her voice every bit as taut and cold as his. 'Then perhaps you could consult your diary and pencil me in for a day when it *would* be convenient.'

And before he could reply she walked into his consulting room and slammed the door shut.

The menopause. He had the nerve to suggest that her tiredness and irritability might be due to the menopause. That would teach her to marry a gynaecologist. One mention of being tired and fed up, and her husband's mind had immediately gone into diagnostic mode.

Well, his mind could just come right out of diagnostic mode, she decided, sitting angrily down at his desk. She might not have known how aggrieved she'd been feeling, but now that she did know she could see it was time he pulled his weight at home—way past time.

And way past time for her clinic to start, she realised

with a muttered oath as she caught sight of the clock on the wall.

'Forget it, Helen,' she told herself, pulling the stack of files on the desk towards her and hitting the intercom button. 'Think about it later, but right now forget it.'

And she managed to until her last patient turned out to be Jennifer Norton.

'I'm feeling fine, thank you, Doctor,' Jennifer said as she eased herself up onto the examination table. 'In fact, now I've got over the morning sickness, the only thing I want is for my husband to stop fussing over me.'

Lucky you, Helen thought, but she didn't say that.

'You can't really blame him for fussing,' she said instead, wrapping the blood-pressure cuff round Jennifer's arm. 'You gave us all a big fright back in February.'

Jennifer had. At just eight weeks pregnant she'd been rushed into the department with vaginal bleeding, and as her pregnancy was the result of her fourth IVF treatment the signs weren't good. Luckily the bleeding had stopped, but Jennifer still had a long way to go.

'You're fourteen weeks pregnant now, aren't you?' she murmured, watching the blood-pressure gauge.

'Fourteen weeks gone, only another twenty-six to go.' Jennifer laughed a little nervously. 'Is it OK—my blood pressure?'

'It's up a little, but that might just be because you knew you were going to be examined today. Unless you've been doing something really silly, of course, like redecorating the whole house.'

'Chance would be a fine thing. If I so much as look at a duster my husband's down on me like a ton of bricks, saying I'm doing too much, putting the twins at risk.'

'I'd enjoy the pampering while you can,' Helen said with more of an edge than she'd intended. 'Speaking as the mother of twins myself, you're going to need all the energy you've got once they arrive. Twelve bottles a day to sterilise and prepare. Two dirty bottoms to change. Two little bodies that suddenly sprout six arms and legs when you're trying to get them dressed to go out.'

Jennifer smiled. 'But I bet you never regretted having them.'

'On good days, no. On bad days...' Helen rolled her eyes heavenwards, and Jennifer laughed. 'OK, I see from your notes that you've already had your spina bifida scan, so I just need to take a blood sample and then we'll do a quick scan to check on how your babies are doing.'

To Jennifer's clear relief the scan revealed that the twins were the correct size and development for their gestation.

'I hate having these scans,' she admitted as she wiped the conductive gel off her tummy and pulled up her trousers. 'I know they're necessary, but I'm always terrified you're going to tell me something's wrong.'

'It's understandable to worry after all you've been through,' Helen said gently. 'Now, we'd like to see you again in a month's time—'

'Another scan?'

''Fraid so. Hey, look on the bright side,' Helen continued as Jennifer groaned. 'It will give you the chance to see how much your babies have grown, and we'll be able to check on your blood pressure at the same time.' She flicked through Tom's diary. 'How does the second of May sound?'

'Fine by me. Brian and I aren't exactly living a wild social life at the moment. Not that we were ever great party-goers even before I got pregnant,' Jennifer said ruefully. 'My husband's the original stick-in-the-mud, stay-at-home bloke.'

Helen smiled, but when the woman got to her feet she suddenly said on impulse, 'How long have you been married, Jennifer?'

'Fifteen years. Cripes, that's longer than the average

sentence for murder, isn't it? Not that I've ever felt like murdering him—at least, not often.'

'Husbands do drive you mad sometimes, don't they?' Helen said with feeling.

'And how.' Jennifer nodded. 'In fact, Brian and I went through a really sticky patch a couple of years ago. I thought he was taking me for granted, he thought our marriage was in a rut.'

Which has got absolutely nothing to do with Jennifer's medical condition, Helen told herself firmly, so you can't possibly ask how she solved the problem, but she did, and Jennifer laughed.

'We talked.'

'That's it?' Helen said in surprise.

'The best answers are often the simplest.'

'Yes, but—'

'Talking clears the air, stops things festering. So does accepting neither of you is perfect. If you don't accept that, then you end up like one of these weird film stars, constantly flitting from relationship to relationship, in love with the idea of being in love.'

Jennifer was right. It was silly to be envious of Gideon and Annie. Stupid to let little things annoy her. She loved Tom, and he loved her, and at least he'd noticed something was wrong, which was more than could be said for a lot of men. OK, so his explanation might have been totally off the wall as far as accuracy was concerned, but at least he'd noticed.

Which meant she was going to have to apologise, she realised as she showed Jennifer out. Not for what she'd said—she wasn't going to take a word of that back—but perhaps she could have phrased it better, picked a better time to raise the subject.

She glanced down at her watch and sighed. Time. It was the one thing she never seemed to have enough of, and she didn't have any spare now. Lunch would be yet another quick sandwich in the staffroom, and then it was on to the ward round.

A ward round that did little to improve her spirits or her temper. She didn't mind spending forty minutes with Mrs Alexander—heaven knew, the woman had just cause to be worried about her unborn baby after having suffered a deep-vein thrombosis—but she was in no mood for Mrs Foster's complaint that her hysterectomy stitches wouldn't have burst if they had been inserted properly.

'Some days it just doesn't pay to get up, does it?' Liz Baker, the sister in charge of the Obs and Gynae ward, observed sympathetically when Helen strode towards her, her cheeks red with barely concealed anger.

'Tell me about it,' Helen began. 'That Mrs Foster—'

'Is a pain in the butt.' Liz nodded. 'I know, and I hate to have to add to your problems but Haematology's just been on the phone. Apparently one of the blood samples you took this morning isn't quite right. Look, why don't you use the phone in the staffroom to call them back?' Liz continued as Helen groaned. 'Get yourself a cup of coffee at the same time.'

A cup of coffee sounded good. Something considerably stronger sounded even better, she decided when she left the ward and began walking towards the staffroom, only to see Tom coming towards her.

She came to an uncertain halt. He did, too.

'I'm sorry.'

They'd spoken in unison, and Tom shook his head. 'You have nothing to apologise for, but I obviously do. I hadn't realised I wasn't pulling my weight at home.'

'No, but you get called out a lot more at night than I do,' she replied, more than willing to meet him halfway. 'And I don't have all your departmental meetings.'

'Yes, but I should have noticed you were doing it all. The trouble is I've been so busy, and...' He shook his head. 'No, that's no excuse. Being busy is no excuse for not pulling my weight, and I'm sorry.'

'Hey, we're not heading for the divorce courts over this or anything,' she said gently as he stared at her, his grey eyes troubled. 'All I'm asking for is a little more help around the house and with the children.'

'You've got it,' he said. 'Whatever you want, you've got.'

She chuckled. 'That's dangerous talk, Tom. What if I ask you for the moon?'

His grey eyes softened. 'If you want the moon I'll get you the moon. If you want...' He paused and his face creased into a broad smile of welcome. 'Mark, you old reprobate, you've finally got here.'

Helen glanced over her shoulder, and blinked.

Wow.

Wow, wow and triple wow.

Tom hadn't been exaggerating when he'd said his friend was handsome. In fact, Tom hadn't been nearly fulsome enough, she thought, automatically tucking in her tummy and standing up straighter, only to feel slightly silly afterwards because this was Tom's friend and she didn't need or want to impress him.

But Mark Lorimer was impressive. Tall, and tanned, with thick black hair, and green eyes. Not a wishy-washy anaemic green, but green like sparkling emeralds, and fringed by quite indecently long black eyelashes.

'Helen, this is Mark,' Tom said unnecessarily after he and his friend had indulged in that mutual backslapping routine which heterosexual males always seemed to feel obliged to perform whenever they met a friend they hadn't seen for years. 'Mark, this is my wife, Helen.'

'It's nice to meet you, Mark,' she said, holding out her hand. 'Tom's talked such a lot about you.'

Which wasn't exactly true. In fact, her husband hadn't

mentioned him at all until Rachel Dunwoody had taken compassionate leave, but it hardly seemed polite to say so.

'You've come as a bit of a surprise to me, too.' He grinned, clearly reading her mind. 'Tom never said he was married, but now that I've met you...' his green eyes swept over her '...all I can say is I hope he knows what a very lucky man he is.'

It was flattery, of course. Tom had always said she had the loveliest smile he'd ever seen, and the biggest brown eyes, but she knew her limitations. She wasn't beautiful—not even particularly pretty—and she laughed and shook her head.

'I bet you say that to all the girls.'

'Actually, no, I don't.'

He was still staring at her, still holding her hand, and to her acute embarrassment she realised she was blushing.

Oh, for heaven's sake, pull yourself together, she told herself severely, quickly withdrawing her hand. You're a thirty-two-year-old mother of two, and just because an absolutely jaw-droppingly gorgeous man is smiling at you shouldn't mean that you should start behaving like a dumbstruck teenager.

'The fog's all gone from Heathrow Airport, then?' she said. Oh, jeez, Helen. He'd hardly be standing here if it wasn't, would he? 'I mean—I meant—you must be really tired after all your travelling.'

'Not at all,' he replied. 'But, then, I've always been able to sleep anywhere.'

He certainly didn't look as though he'd just spent goodness knows how many hours on a plane, and then been marooned in an airport. He looked pristine, and immaculate, and she just knew she must look as though she'd been dragged through a hedge backwards, her hair coming loose from her scrunchy, her sweater the first thing that had come to hand that morning.

Not that it mattered, of course. She was a doctor, here to work, but...

'I'm afraid you'll have to excuse me,' she said, beginning to back up the corridor. 'I have blood results to chase up—'

'Hey, you're not abandoning me already, are you?' he protested, and Tom smiled.

'Of course she's not. In fact, I'll make sure Helen takes care of you, shows you the ropes.'

It made sense. Tom was hardly likely to expect Annie to do the honours when she was only a junior doctor, but Helen couldn't help but wish her husband hadn't suggested it.

She wished it even more when she got to the end of the corridor and glanced back. Mark and Tom were deep in conversation, but Mark must have sensed her gaze on him because he suddenly looked up and smiled. A warm, wide smile that sent a disturbing shiver of awareness racing down her spine.

A disturbing shiver that she didn't want to feel.

CHAPTER TWO

GIDEON drummed his fingers absently on top of his desk, then frowned. 'How long has Mrs Alexander been with us now?'

Tom glanced down at his notes. 'A week.'

'OK. As the venogram didn't show any sign of the clot moving, we'll keep her on the heparin until a week on Thursday, then induce her. I know it's risky,' he continued as Tom looked uncertain, 'but to perform a Caesarean on a woman who's had a deep-vein thrombosis...' He shook his head. 'Too much could go wrong.'

'Which brings us to Mrs Foster,' Tom observed. 'She's still complaining about her burst stitches.'

'Mrs Foster should think herself damn lucky she's not in Intensive Care,' Gideon retorted. 'What the hell was she thinking of, straining to pass a motion after major surgery?'

'I know, but she's driving Helen crazy, saying her burst stitches were due to negligence, sloppy surgery...'

'I'll have a word with her.' The corners of the consultant's lips quirked. 'Better yet, why don't I get Mark to have a word with her? He's supposed to have quite a way with the ladies, isn't he?'

Apart from with Helen, Tom thought with a slight frown. Obs and Gynae might have been inundated with nurses suddenly discovering an urgent need to visit the ward since Mark's arrival a week ago, but Helen had remained strangely reticent whenever he'd asked how she was getting on with him.

'He *is* a good doctor, isn't he?' Gideon continued,

clearly misinterpreting the frown. 'I mean, I'm not employing him simply to sweet-talk difficult patients...'

'He's one of the best,' Tom reassured him. 'He might be the most terrible flirt, but what he doesn't know about Obs and Gynae could be written on a postage stamp.'

Gideon looked relieved. 'In that case, I wish we could employ him permanently instead of for just six weeks. Oh, I know he wouldn't accept a longer contract with us even if we could offer it,' he continued when Tom made to interrupt. 'Nobody in their right mind would swap a job in Canada for one at the Belfield, but—'

'We need him.' Tom nodded. 'Even if Rachel was back we'd still need him. I take it Admin still won't agree to us advertising for another member of staff?'

'Admin says what it always says. Until the hospital gets more funding we're to manage as best we can. It's the old story. Live long enough, old horse, and eventually you might get hay.'

Tom laughed. 'I've never thought of myself as an old horse, but now you come to mention it...'

'Yup, beasts of burden, that's us. And speaking of being overworked....' Gideon picked up one of the files on his desk, then put it down again. 'I don't want you to think I'm being nosy, or interfering where I'm not wanted, but Annie was saying...'

'Annie was saying?' Tom repeated blankly as the consultant came to an obviously embarrassed halt.

'Well, you know what women are like, Tom,' Gideon said in a rush, 'and she's probably got it all wrong, but she was saying to me the other day that she thought Helen looked a bit down, a bit depressed.'

Annie had noticed? Annie, who had been at the Belfield for less than four months, had noticed? Tom bit his lip. Dammit, he should have been the first one to see there was a problem, and yet he hadn't. Maybe women were better attuned to picking up on that sort of thing than men, or maybe he was just insensitive. It wasn't a comforting thought.

'Helen's fine,' he murmured. 'Just tired, like the rest of us.'

Probably more so since he'd been helping out at home, he thought ruefully, but how was he supposed to know that the little round symbol with the cross through it meant, Do not tumble-dry?

'Hell, I should have been in Theatre ten minutes ago,' Gideon exclaimed, quickly getting to his feet only to pause, his eyebrows raised. 'Unless there's something else you want to discuss with me?'

For a moment Tom hesitated, then shook his head. The consultant might be his friend as well as his boss, but some things were private, and revealing that Helen had accused him of not pulling his weight definitely came under the heading of private.

He was running late, too. Rhona Scott was booked in for an outpatient hysterosalpingogram this morning, and though he'd asked Helen to prepare her for him it wasn't fair to keep either of them waiting. Rhona was a natural born worrier, and as for Helen…the last thing he wanted was to give her another opportunity to accuse him of taking advantage of her.

No, that wasn't fair, he thought with a deep sigh as he strode down the corridor towards his consulting room. It had clearly taken a lot to make her say what she had, but why on earth hadn't she said something before? OK, so maybe he'd never been much of a New Age man, but neither was he a mind-reader.

'Problems?' Helen said, seeing his frown when he opened the door of his consulting room to find Rhona Scott already prepared and waiting.

'No more than usual,' he replied irritably, only to groan when he saw Helen stiffen. Why the hell had he said that? He hadn't meant to sound so snippy, but there was nothing he could do about it—not with Mrs Scott staring curiously at him. 'All set for your hysterosalpingogram, Rhona?' he said instead.

'To be honest, no,' she said. 'Call me chicken, but the thought of you putting some dye up into me…' She shuddered. 'Are you absolutely sure I can't have an anaesthetic?'

He shook his head. 'I'm afraid the only way we can get really good X-ray pictures of the insides of your Fallopian tubes, and find out why you're having such difficulty getting pregnant, is to carry out the procedure while you're wide awake. It won't hurt,' he added, seeing her flinch when he picked up the small tube. 'You may feel a momentary discomfort when I insert the dye into your uterus, but I promise that's all you're going to feel.'

Rhona didn't look convinced and out of the corner of his eye he saw Helen reach out and catch hold of her hand.

She'd always been much better at dealing with patients—people—than he was. Maybe it was another female thing, but he'd always found it a lot harder to get the right blend of sympathy and understanding, and he could still get it wrong.

Very badly wrong, he thought, remembering how angry Helen had been when he'd suggested she might be going through an early menopause. Well, OK, so his diagnosis might not have been the right one but, dammit, he'd been worried about her. He still was.

It was all very well for her to keep on saying she was simply tired, and if she had more help at home everything would be fine, but he couldn't rid himself of the nagging feeling that there was more to it than that. Something he was missing, but what the 'something' might be was beyond him.

'Dr Brooke?'

Helen's eyes were on him, clearly wondering why he hadn't started the procedure, and he flushed slightly.

'Just checking the dosage,' he lied, but she didn't buy it. He hadn't really expected her to. After ten years of marriage, she could read him like a book. He'd once thought he could do the same with her, but recently... 'Ready, Rhona?' he said, forcing his mind back to the present with difficulty.

She nodded nervously, and as carefully and gently as he could he began inserting the tube into her cervix through her vagina.

'It'll all be over in a second.' Helen smiled reassuringly down at the woman. 'Once the dye is in your uterus it will show up white on a special screen we have, and after we've taken a few X-rays you can go home.'

'Will I get the results today?'

'I'm afraid not,' Tom replied. 'We have to process and examine them first, you see.' Not to mention being so damn swamped with patients that we just don't have the time, he added mentally. 'But I'll get our secretary to make an appointment for you to come in and see me on Friday, if that's OK?'

Rhona nodded.

'Not much more to go now,' Helen declared. 'Just keep on relaxing. Good, Rhona... Well done... That's it.'

'The dye's in?' the woman exclaimed. 'But I didn't feel anything.'

'I'd have hung up my stethoscope if you had.' Tom smiled. 'OK, all I want you to do now is to lie as still as you can while our technician takes the pictures.'

'I should have got my hair done for the occasion, shouldn't I?' Rhona said with a shaky laugh, and he chuckled and patted her shoulder.

'You look fine.'

Her X-rays, unfortunately, didn't.

'No wonder she hasn't been able to conceive,' Helen observed. 'That swelling where her right Fallopian tube joins her uterus—it means the tube is completely blocked, doesn't it?'

'It looks like it,' Tom replied. 'If the blockage hasn't extended right through the uterine wall I could certainly perform a cornual anastomosis—cutting out the blocked section of the Fallopian tube and rejoining it—but…'

'Our theatre schedule's so full it's anybody's guess as to when Rhona could have the operation,' she finished for him.

Tom nodded, then frowned. 'I'm going to pull strings on this one. It's crazy for her to have to wait when we've got somebody of Mark's calibre on the team.'

'Mark has experience of tubal surgery?' she exclaimed. 'I didn't know that.'

'Oh, there's lots of things you don't know about me.' A deep male voice chuckled, and Tom saw his wife jump as though somebody had lit a firecracker behind her.

'Haven't you ever heard of knocking?' she said. 'Creeping up on people like that. Is there something wrong on the ward?'

'Apart from the fact that you're not there?' Mark grinned. 'Not a thing.'

Tom wryly shook his head as he saw a deep flush of colour cross his wife's cheeks. Same old Mark. Still couldn't resist turning on the charm, flirting with every woman he met. Helen didn't appear to appreciate it, though. In fact, she looked angry, tense, and deftly he steered Mark towards the X-rays.

'OK, earn your salary. Take a look at this.'

Mark stared at the screen. 'Somebody's uterus, right?'

'No, somebody's left foot,' Tom responded. 'Cut the jokes, Mark—tell me what you think.'

'That right Fallopian tube—it could simply be scarred, but…' He shook his head. 'Blocked, I'd say, but the clarity's not very good. What did you take the pictures with— an old box Brownie camera?'

'Mark.'

He grinned. 'OK—OK. Probably blocked, perhaps due to an infection caused by a coil. How old is your patient?'

'Thirty-six. Married for eight years, and been trying for a baby for the last six.'

'And she's only just having an exploratory hysterosalpingogram now?' Mark gasped. 'Jeez, what the hell have you guys been doing for the past five years?'

'Working our way through a very long waiting list,' Helen snapped before Tom could say anything. 'The Belfield doesn't have a separate infertility clinic, so we treat people as and when we can. Rhona only got onto our list last year—'

'But—'

'Look, we do the best we can, OK?' Helen said impatiently, and Mark sighed.

'Well, all I can say is things are very different in Australia.'

Helen muttered something which sounded suspiciously like, 'So how come you didn't stay there?' and Tom shot her a puzzled glance.

He was the one who usually got angry and frustrated, dealing with the limitations of the service they could offer, but Helen hadn't sounded simply angry, she'd sounded positively antagonistic.

Awkwardly he cleared his throat. 'I don't know what happens in Australia, but under the NHS there's a nine-month to a year waiting list for non-urgent surgery, and a cornual anastomosis is considered non-urgent. I know,' he said as Mark's eyebrows shot up, 'but that's how it is.'

'Then why the hell do you put up with it?' Mark demanded. 'Dammit, Tom, you're a first-rate surgeon. If you went to Oz, or to the States, you could be head of your own department, and not have to put up with this sort of crap.'

'Perhaps,' Tom said, 'but Helen and I like the Belfield. It's where we met, and we've a fondness for the old place.'

'Which doesn't mean we're always going to stay here,' Helen said swiftly. 'I mean, who's to say what's round the corner for any of us—what changes we might make?'

Mark glanced from her to Tom thoughtfully. 'So it's only old Tom who's reluctant to move, is it? You always did play it too safe, mate.'

'Whether I do or whether I don't is immaterial,' Tom replied, wondering what on earth had made Helen say what she had, and not liking the reference to himself as 'old' either. 'Mrs Scott is certainly not going to have to wait nine months when we've got someone with your experience on the team. I'll have a word with Gideon, insist we get her in while you're here to help me.'

'In that case, I'd better take a closer look at these X-rays,' Mark said. 'If we're going to be operating on this lady, I want as much information as I can get.'

Tom nodded but he couldn't help but notice that when Mark moved closer to the screen, Helen instantly stepped back.

'If you don't need me any longer I have a mass of paperwork to catch up on,' she said. 'Not to mention my antenatal clinic in an hour.'

She was already heading for the door, and Tom quickly followed her. 'Thanks for holding the fort for me, love. I really appreciate it.'

She smiled up at him, but she didn't even so much as glance in Mark's direction as she left, and Mark's eyebrows rose.

'Whoa, but did it suddenly get distinctly chilly in here, or what?'

'I'm not surprised,' Tom observed tightly. 'Criticising our department and its equipment wasn't exactly the smartest thing in the world to do.'

'Just telling it like it is,' Mark replied. 'It's not my fault if Helen is hypersensitive to criticism. In fact…' He came to a halt as he encountered a look in Tom's eyes. A look he'd never seen before. A look that held neither warmth nor amusement, and he held up his hands defensively. 'Hey, no offence meant, mate. Look, I'll apologise to her, OK?'

'Do that,' Tom declared, his grey eyes hard, cold. 'I don't like my wife upset, and I won't have her upset. Not by you, not by anyone.'

Mark stared at him for a second. 'Tom the protector. Tom the defender. You've changed since our med days, haven't you?'

'If you mean I've grown up—realised what and who is important in my life—then, yes, I've changed,' Tom replied. 'Helen is more important to me than my job, this hospital and our friendship, and you'd be well advised never to forget that.'

Mark grinned. 'Whoops, but I've suddenly got that chilly feeling again. Look, I've said I'll apologise,' he continued as Tom's eyebrows snapped together. 'I'll even grovel if I have to. Satisfied now?'

Tom nodded. 'Mark, listen—'

'Helen doesn't seem to like me very much, does she?'

Helen didn't appear to, but there was no way Tom was going to agree. 'Helen likes everyone,' he said evasively.

'OK, let's just say I'm not feeling the love,' Mark observed, and Tom couldn't help but laugh.

'The trouble with you, my friend, is that far too many women have been bowled over by your charm over the years, and it's a blow to your ego when one isn't.'

'You reckon?'

'I reckon,' Tom confirmed. 'In fact, I think it's high time you settled down.'

'And deny all the lovely women out there the pleasure of my company? No way.'

'Maybe that kind of attitude is OK when you're in your

twenties,' Tom said, horribly aware that he suddenly felt very old, 'but you're thirty-four—'

'So I should be looking for a woman to settle down with,' Mark completed for him in a mock-sonorous tone. 'Perhaps I would if all the best ones weren't already taken.' One corner of his mouth turned up. 'Women like your Helen. Now, if I'd met her before I went to Oz—'

'You wouldn't have stood a chance.' Tom laughed. 'It was love at first sight for Helen and me.'

It had been, and the love was still there, he thought as he began labelling the X-rays and putting them into Rhona Scott's file. Even now she could still make his pulses race simply by smiling at him. Even now he felt a tightness round his heart when he saw her coming out of the shower, her hair all tousled, her skin pink and glowing.

He glanced thoughtfully across at Mark. When they'd been students he'd always envied Mark his good looks and easy charm, but he didn't envy him now. Flitting from woman to woman, moving on when he got bored or if some other female caught his eye. It was an empty sort of a life, rootless and ultimately unsatisfying.

No, he didn't envy Mark. He had a wife who loved him, two wonderful children, whereas Mark... Mark had absolutely nothing that he wanted any more.

'He's gorgeous, isn't he?' Liz Baker said dreamily as she switched on the staffroom kettle. 'His thick black hair, his tan, those eyes...'

'Looks aren't everything,' Helen interrupted tersely. 'In fact, give me an honest, ordinary-looking man any day of the week.'

'Hear! hear!' Annie agreed.

'Mark Lorimer,' Liz continued, as though neither of them had spoken. 'Even his name sounds romantic, don't you think? Like something out of a story book.'

'*Grimm's Fairy Tales*, perhaps?' Helen suggested, and Liz looked momentarily startled, then laughed.

'Oh, come on, Helen, you're not telling me you don't think he's seriously attractive?'

He was, but that didn't give him the right to waltz into the Belfield and criticise the way they worked, Helen thought, unwrapping her sandwiches with more vigour than was strictly necessary. Neither did it give him the right to imply that she and Tom were a pair of old stick-in-the-muds with no ambition because they'd never worked anywhere else. They had children, for heaven's sake—obligations. Something that Mark Lorimer clearly knew nothing about.

'Madge in Paediatrics thinks he's handsome,' Liz continued. 'So does Phyllis in Radiography—'

'Madge and Phyllis should stop behaving like a pair of silly moon-struck schoolgirls,' Helen retorted, then bit her lip when Liz's mouth fell open.

Oh, Lord, but that had been an incredibly bitchy thing to say. Even Annie clearly thought it was, judging by the way she was staring at her, but she was sick to death of everybody giggling over Mark Lorimer like he was a film star or something.

Yes, he was quite unbelievably good-looking. Yes, he had a voice that could melt butter, and eyes that seemed to gaze down deep inside you, but anyone with half a brain should also have been able to see that he was also an unprincipled flirt. Good grief, put him in front of any female between the ages of eight and eighty—herself included—and he instantly switched on the charm.

Well, she wasn't some naïve schoolgirl who could be impressed by a few slick words, a few finely tuned compliments, she thought with irritation as the staffroom door opened, and Mark came in, deep in conversation with Tom and Gideon. She was more interested in whether he was any good as a doctor.

'Good news, Helen,' Tom declared, coming over to sit beside her. 'Gideon's agreed to slot Rhona Scott in for surgery as quickly as possible, and we've got two possible dates. One for Monday the week after next, and the other for the end of May.'

'Rhona would come in this afternoon if you asked her,' Helen murmured, taking a bite out of her sandwich and trying very hard to ignore the fact that Mark was flirting quite outrageously with Liz.

'You don't think she might feel both dates are too soon?' Tom said. 'We're talking major surgery here, and she'll be in hospital for at least a week. As she's a school-teacher she might prefer to wait until the long summer holidays.'

'Trust me, she won't.'

'Female intuition?' her husband said curiously.

'Female heart.' She smiled.

'OK, that's good enough for me. I'll suggest the Monday when she comes in for the results of her hyster-osalpingogram, and see what she says.'

Helen nodded. Annie was getting ready to go off duty, and she saw Gideon bend his head to catch something his wife had said, then laugh and press her hand briefly to his lips.

She and Tom used to do that, Helen thought wistfully. Steal kisses, hold hands simply for the pleasure of touching one another. In fact, they'd joked that there wasn't a sluice room in the hospital they hadn't used at one time or another for a secret rendezvous.

And I'm doing it again, she thought angrily as the couple left the staffroom. Envying them, and it's so *stupid*. The love I feel for Tom is bound to have changed over the years, become less intense, more familiar, more comfortable.

Like a pair of old slippers, her mind whispered, and she shook her head. No, not like an old pair of slippers.

She loved Tom, and he loved her. Their love was just...different now.

'I'll see you later, then.'

'You're going?' she exclaimed, seeing her husband get to his feet. 'But you haven't had any lunch.'

'No time. Admin wants a word with Gideon about Mark's work permit so I'm stuck babysitting his students.' He half started towards the door, then turned. 'Which reminds me. Gideon was a bit worried about his afternoon ward round, so I said you'd help Mark to do it.'

Oh, brilliant, Tom, she thought vexedly as he strode away. Like you couldn't perhaps have checked with me first—asked if it was OK? I'm still only halfway through my paperwork because I was helping you this morning, and now you've gone and lost me this afternoon as well.

'He really shouldn't have done that,' Mark murmured, slipping into the seat Tom had vacated. 'Just assumed you'd help me.'

She couldn't agree more, but there was no way she was going to say so.

'He's the specialist registrar, I'm an SHO—it's his job to allocate work,' she said defensively, wishing that Liz would come over and join them, but she was busy on the phone.

'But shouldn't he have checked you with first, rather than simply say you'd do it?'

'Like I said, it's his job,' she repeated, and his mouth turned up at the corners.

'And as he's also your husband you're damned if you're going to bad-mouth him to a semi-stranger.'

It was so exactly what she'd been thinking that Helen couldn't prevent an involuntary chuckle springing to her lips, and his smile widened.

'That's better. I was beginning to think I was going to be put in the dog-house for the duration after what I said about Rhona Scott's treatment this morning.'

She stared down at the remains of her sandwich, then sighed. 'I know things are far from perfect at the Belfield, but—'

'You don't want—or need—some big-mouth newcomer like me telling you so,' he finished for her.

She couldn't deny it. Not when his eyes were brimming with laughter, and warmth, and something else which was making her heart race, her breathing jerky and erratic.

He's flirting with you, she told herself, trying to look away, only to find that she couldn't. He does it with everyone, and you're a big girl, you can handle it.

But she couldn't and that, she realised, was the trouble. She could tell herself—and anybody else who cared to listen—that Mark Lorimer was nothing but a womaniser, and she was more interested in his qualifications than in him, but it wasn't true. The plain, galling truth was that she was as impressed and stunned by him as every other woman in the Belfield.

Dammit, she'd actually caught herself choosing clothes to wear to work now instead of just grabbing whatever was nearest, and yesterday she'd found herself looking at lipsticks and eye shadows in the chemist. And it was crazy.

She was married. She was *happily* married, and even if Mark Lorimer was the handsomest, sexiest man in the world, her knees shouldn't be turning to water and her brain to mush whenever he smiled at her. And they were.

'Helen?'

Oh, Lord, could he possibly know what she was thinking? There was certainly a decidedly wicked-looking gleam in his eyes, and she stood up fast. 'I…I'm afraid you'll have to excuse me. I want…I need to have a word with Liz.'

He didn't believe her. She could tell by the way he smiled that he didn't, but she didn't care. All she wanted was to be as far away from him, and her own unsettling thoughts and feelings, as she could possibly get.

'The agency can't supply me with any emergency nursing cover for this afternoon,' Liz declared, slamming down the staffroom phone. 'Apparently I haven't given them enough notice. Not enough notice,' she repeated furiously. 'Like how exactly am I supposed to know when people are going to be sick?'

And how could I have predicted I'd start behaving like a loopy schoolgirl because a handsome man keeps smiling at me? Helen thought unhappily.

'Is there anything I can do to help?' she asked as Liz made for the door.

The sister shook her head. 'All I can do is phone around, and see if I can sweet-talk somebody into coming in on their day off.'

Helen wished she had the day off, too, when Liz had gone and she turned to find Mark staring at her thoughtfully.

'We'd better get going,' she began. 'We're doing Gideon's ward round, remember, and—'

'You don't like me very much, do you?' he observed.

Whatever else she might have been expecting him to say, it hadn't been that, and she flushed.

'I don't know you well enough to dislike you,' she said, striving to sound light, dismissive, which wasn't easy with a pair of intense green eyes fixed on her.

'That's what I figured.' He nodded. 'In fact, it might surprise you to know that I'm generally considered to be quite likable.'

It didn't surprise her in the least. Men who were as charming and handsome as Mark Lorimer were generally well liked. In fact, if she was honest—and she had absolutely no intention of being honest—she would have admitted that she could all too easily get to like him herself. A lot.

'I really do think we should start making tracks,' she

said uncomfortably. 'The ward's pretty full so it will take us quite a while.'

'Tom tells me you have eight-year-old twins—Emma and John?' he said, clasping his hands behind his head and leaning back in his seat. 'They must be quite a handful.'

'They have their moments,' she replied, wondering what else Tom might have told him, and just where this conversation was going.

'It must be very difficult for you—holding down a full-time job, running a home, looking after your kids.'

'Tom does his share,' she said swiftly. Well, he'd been trying to recently, she told herself, though at the moment his efforts were proving more of a hindrance than a help. 'It's not a solo effort.'

'I can't imagine Tom as a New Age man.'

He hadn't make it sound like a compliment. In fact, he'd somehow managed to make Tom sound both boring and dull, and before she could stop herself she said, 'I don't know about New Age, but he's certainly a lot more adult than men who flit from girlfriend to girlfriend, with no roots or purpose in life.'

Mark grinned. 'I've no doubt he is. But I bet he's not nearly so exciting.'

There was no answer to that—at least none she could immediately think of—and she strode to the staffroom door and opened it. 'Our ward round, Dr Lorimer?'

'Didn't think he was,' he said, his green eyes dancing.

And you're too smart by half, Helen thought as she followed him down the corridor. Too smart, too charming, too everything.

Well, maybe he wouldn't be quite so smart and charming after a couple of hours on the ward, she thought waspishly. Maybe a couple of hours of examinations, blood pressures and sheer exhausting hard work, would dent his charm and overweening confidence.

It didn't. Not even when Mrs Foster launched into her

usual round of complaints the minute he appeared at her bedside.

'A week is how long I was told I'd be in here,' she declared, her beady eyes sweeping over him with no appearance of being in the least impressed. 'One week, and now no one can tell me when I'm going home. If my stitches had been inserted properly—'

'The trouble is, you tried to go to the toilet too soon after your hysterectomy,' Mark interrupted, his face a picture of warm solicitude. 'I can understand why you wanted to—an active, independent person like yourself—'

'Well, I've never been lazy,' she said, her eyes softening slightly, 'but—'

'And I appreciate that you're anxious to go home, what with having little ones to take care of…'

'My youngest is twenty-five.'

'Good grief, you must have been married very young,' he exclaimed. 'I wouldn't have put you a day over forty.'

Mrs Foster pinkened, and simpered. 'Well, I've always tried to take care of myself, but—'

'And that's what we want to do for you now,' he continued with a dazzling smile. 'Take care of you. *I* want to take care of you, and surely you're not going to deny me that opportunity, or the pleasure of your company?'

Helen heard Liz choke behind her, and she only just managed to maintain her own composure by staring determinedly at the wall over Mrs Foster's bed, but when Mark had moved on down the ward she couldn't restrain her laughter.

'That was the most outrageous example of flattery I've ever heard,' she gasped.

'It worked, though, didn't it?' he protested. 'And you're not telling me that dreadful woman hasn't been a thorn in your side for the past week.'

'No, but—'

'And it got you to smile at me, instead of shooting daggers, so it was worth it.'

Mark's eyes were deep, and warm, and she shook her head. 'You're completely incorrigible.'

'But likable?' he suggested, and she shook her head again, and laughed.

He *was* likable. Dangerously likable. In fact, in the space of a week he had somehow managed to make her feel more feminine, more attractive and more desirable than she had done in years, and it had to stop.

She had to start distancing herself from this man. For her own peace of mind and safety she needed to distance herself from him, or…

Don't go that way, her mind warned. You're married, and he's Tom's friend, so don't let your mind go down that road even for a second.

'Helen?'

A smile was playing about his lips, and again she had that uncanny feeling again that he was reading her mind.

Abruptly she turned on her heel. 'We've two more patients left to see. Which do you want first—Mrs Alexander or Mrs White?'

CHAPTER THREE

'ANYTHING happening yet?' Helen murmured, hovering at the delivery room door while Liz checked Mary Alexander's blood pressure, then the foetal monitor.

'Nothing,' Tom muttered back. 'I'm afraid it looks like we're going to have to go for the Caesarean after all.'

Helen nodded. Tom had ruptured Mary Alexander's membrane earlier in the morning to release some of the amniotic fluid around the baby. In theory that should have induced her contractions, but when nothing had happened he'd ordered an IV line of oxytocin, and yet still there was no sign of her going into labour.

'BP up, foetal heartbeat becoming a little unsteady,' Liz said in an undertone.

'Shouldn't something be happening by now, Doctor?' Mary asked, gazing uncertainly up at Tom. 'I know I'm no expert, but—'

'Occasionally we get a baby who's reluctant to leave the nice warm shelter of his mummy's tummy.' He smiled, his face a picture of calm, controlled confidence. 'It's nothing to worry about.'

But it's taking too long, Helen thought, seeing the concern behind her husband's bright façade. With so much of the amniotic fluid gone the baby was going to be in big trouble soon if they didn't do something.

Tom met her eyes and he nodded. It was time to alert the theatre staff.

'Do you want me to page Gideon, tell him what's happening?' she asked after she'd phoned the theatre and Tom had explained the situation to Mary and her husband.

'Please. A Caesarean's the one thing he was hoping to

avoid after her deep-vein thrombosis, but...' He sighed wryly as one of their porters wheeled a very frightened-looking Mary and her husband out of the delivery room. 'Want to wish me luck?'

'You won't need it,' she declared, and he smiled.

'Female intuition?'

'Professional opinion,' she replied, and he shook his head and laughed as he hurried after Mary, but she meant it. He might not have Mark's flamboyance when it came to operating, but he was good—very good.

And Annie looked decidedly harassed when Helen met her coming out of the ward.

'Tell me that you speak Greek,' the junior doctor exclaimed. 'Please—*please*—tell me you speak Greek.'

'Why in the world would—?'

'It's Mrs Dukakis. She came into A and E this morning complaining of severe stomach pains. They decided she was simply suffering from a bad case of indigestion, but when they tried to discharge her she became hysterical so they sent her up to us.'

'But—'

'She's six months pregnant, and...' Annie shook her head. 'Look, come and see for yourself. Or, to be more strictly accurate, come and listen.'

Helen did.

'Cripes,' she murmured when Mrs Dukakis finally subsided into silence after a long and virtually incomprehensible account of what she thought was wrong with her.

'Exactly.' Annie nodded. 'Now you see why I was hoping you might speak Greek.'

'I don't, and I'm afraid I can't think of anybody on the staff who does,' Helen replied, seeing Mrs Dukakis gaze uncomprehendingly from her to Annie.

'I believe Mark does,' Liz announced, overhearing them as she passed by with the drugs trolley.

Mark would, Helen thought sourly. Mark probably

spoke ten languages, had an IQ of two million and did rocket science in his spare time.

No, that wasn't fair, she told herself, but after spending the better part of the last ten days trying to avoid him, the last thing she wanted was to actively go looking for him.

'Helen?'

Annie was staring at her curiously, and she forced a smile to her lips. 'We'd better get Mark.'

Mrs Dukakis clearly agreed. In fact, her face lit up like a beacon when he spoke to her in her own language, but something was obviously very badly wrong judging by the number of times she burst into tears when he questioned, then examined her.

'What is it—what's wrong?' Helen asked as Mark took her by the elbow and steered her to the bottom of the ward, leaving Annie to comfort the woman.

'At the moment nothing more drastic than a very bad case of indigestion, but…' He shook his head. 'What do you know about thalassaemia major?'

'That it's a serious, inherited childhood anaemia, most commonly found in people of Mediterranean or Asian descent.' Helen glanced over her shoulder at the sobbing woman. 'Is that why Mrs Dukakis is so upset—is she a thalassaemia carrier?'

'Mrs Dukakis hadn't even heard of the condition until I asked her whether she had any other children,' Mark said grimly. 'She thought she was having a miscarriage.'

'But—'

'Helen, she only came to Glasgow four months ago. Before that she and her husband lived in a poor, very isolated part of Greece with limited medical facilities. All she knows is she's given birth to two other children, and neither of them reached their second birthday. The wasting disease, the people in her village called it.'

What must it be like to lose two children? Helen wondered, staring at Nana Dukakis. To feel them grow inside you, feel them move, then give birth to them, only for them to die so quickly. It didn't bear thinking of.

'It's too late to take a sample from the baby's umbilical cord to find out if it has thalassaemia major, isn't it?' she murmured. 'If she'd known she was a carrier when she first arrived in Glasgow we could have done the test, then offered her a termination, but at six months pregnant...'

'It's too late, but there's still a lot we can do,' Mark declared, his green eyes encouraging. 'First we need to test her and her husband to find out if they're both carriers. If her husband's not, this baby might be all right, and even if it isn't we can start giving it monthly blood transfusions as soon as it's born, and regular injections of Desferal to ensure its liver and kidneys aren't damaged.'

Regular blood transfusions and injections of Desferal. It sounded a wretched life for a little baby, and Mark must have read her thoughts because he smiled. A small, rueful smile.

'It's better than the alternative, Helen, and new treatments are being tried out all the time. We're getting excellent results from bone-marrow transplants, and there's also a lot of work being done with gene therapy.'

He was right, she knew he was, and it was stupid of her to be thinking so negatively. 'What have you told her?'

'The truth. There was no point in skirting round the subject, so I told her I thought her other children had died because they had thalassaemia major, but if we started treating her baby as soon as it was born there was a very good chance it could live to be as old as you or I.'

Helen nodded, then sighed as more immediate concerns suddenly occurred to her. 'You know we can't possibly keep her in—not for indigestion.'

'I'm going to sweet-talk Admissions, ask if she can at least stay for the night. It will give her time to calm down, and me the chance to run some tests.'

'It's going to take some real sweet-talking,' Helen commented. 'We're wall-to-wall patients at the moment.'

He grinned. 'You don't think I'm up to it?'

Oh, he was up to it all right, she thought. In fact, if he treated the women who worked in Admissions to one of his blinding smiles they'd probably agree to Mrs Dukakis staying in one of their private rooms for the duration of her pregnancy.

'Actually, you might not have to talk to Admissions,' Annie said, overhearing the last of their conversation as she joined them. 'Mrs Foster went home this morning—'

'Hallelujah!'

'And Rhona Scott's not due in for her cornual anastomosis until Monday—'

'So unless an emergency comes in we've got a vacant bed for the next few days.' Mark's eyes lit up. 'Liz could OK it for me, couldn't she?'

'Yes, but—'

'Oh, Liz, light of my life, joy of my heart,' he exclaimed, heading off towards the sister before either of them could stop him. 'Could I have a word?'

Annie shook her head as she watched him go. 'He's quite something, isn't he? Handsome, charming and about as reliable as a fifty-pence watch.'

'You reckon?' Helen murmured, seeing Liz frown, then nod, then dissolve into helpless laughter when Mark kissed her soundly on the cheek.

'Don't you?'

There was a very decided edge to the junior doctor's voice, and Helen glanced back at her thoughtfully. She'd never asked—had never thought it was her business to ask—why Annie hadn't married her son's father, but now she thought she knew.

'Annie—'

'I just hope he doesn't break too many hearts while he's here,' the woman continued. 'I'd hate to think of somebody getting hurt—really hurt—because they believe all his flattery.'

Well, I don't, Helen thought firmly, suddenly aware that Annie's eyes were fixed on her. OK, so maybe my heart keeps doing these funny little back flips whenever he smiles at me, and my legs feel odd and strangely wobbly if I meet him unexpectedly, but that's just because he's so darned handsome. It doesn't mean that I'm starting to fall for his charm. It *doesn't*.

It didn't take Liz long to get Nana Dukakis settled in, and when Mr Dukakis arrived he thankfully turned out to speak considerably better English than his wife, but Helen didn't envy Mark the task of asking him if he'd be prepared to give some blood samples.

'At least we can start giving this baby treatment right away if it *is* born with thalassaemia major,' Tom said when Helen told him about it later. 'And the earlier the treatment begins the more chance it will have of surviving.'

Helen nodded as they walked together down the corridor. 'How's Mrs Alexander?'

'Both mum and daughter are doing well. She'll have to go back on the heparin tomorrow, of course, and keep taking it for at least six weeks, but thankfully the clot looks as though it's beginning to disperse and she's going home with a healthy baby girl.'

He should have looked pleased, and yet she thought he looked tired and strained, and she put her hand on his arm. 'Want to share?'

It was what they'd said to one another when they'd first married, and to her surprise he suddenly drew her gently into his arms and rested his chin on her head with a sigh.

'Mary Alexander's clot—Mrs Dukakis's thalassaemia. So many things can go wrong before, during and after, childbirth, Helen, and this afternoon, when I was holding Mary's baby, I thought...'

'What?' she pressed as his voice trailed away into silence. 'What did you think?'

'I found myself remembering the day Emma and John were born.' He shook his head. 'I don't think I've ever been more scared. Scared of losing them, of losing you.'

'You didn't show it,' she said, and he smiled.

'It would have been a terrific confidence-booster for you, wouldn't it, if I'd suddenly got down on my knees in the delivery room and started to pray while you were huffing and puffing?'

She laughed. 'I guess so, but why didn't you tell me afterwards?'

'You'd have thought I was stupid.'

'Of course I wouldn't,' she protested.

'Well, I thought I was stupid,' he declared gruffly. 'I mean, men are supposed to be strong at a time like that, aren't they? Not falling apart like I was, wishing it was me going through the pain, not you, and...' He coloured slightly. 'I'm not very good at saying things, at putting my feelings into words.'

It was true, he wasn't. He'd never been able to make flowery speeches—had great difficulty making any kind of speech at all—and she hugged him tightly.

'Tom Brooke, there are times when you drive me nuts, but I do love you.'

'And I—'

'Tom, Haematology's being a real pain, saying they can't test the blood samples I've taken from Mrs Dukakis really quickly,' Mark said as he came round the corner. 'How do I twist their arm?'

'You can't,' Tom replied, then his lips quirked. 'But Helen could.'

'Tom, don't—'

'Our head of Haematology has been fond of Helen ever since she was a med student,' he continued, to her acute discomfort. 'So whatever Helen wants, Helen gets.'

'Really?' Mark said. 'Now, that's what I'd call a really useful boyfriend.'

'He's not my boyfriend,' she protested. 'He's a grandfather of four, and a very nice man.'

'With impeccable taste.'

Don't do this to me, she thought unhappily as his eyes caught and held hers. Don't look at me like you think I'm fascinating, and interesting, and…and desirable, because I might start to believe you mean it, and I don't want to believe it. It's too dangerous for me to believe it.

'I don't suppose you could possibly pop down to Haematology, could you?' Mark continued. 'Bat your lovely eyelashes at the boss and speed up my results?'

'I'm just going off duty—'

'It wouldn't take you a minute, love,' Tom declared, 'and it would help Mark.'

It took all of Helen's self-control not to turn round and hit him. Couldn't he see that she didn't want to be useful to Mark, didn't want anything to do with Mark?

No, he obviously couldn't, she thought with frustration. He was clearly expecting her to agree, and if she refused he'd wonder what on earth was wrong with her. Might even offer to take her pulse, feel her forehead, then send her home with an aspirin.

And maybe that was what she needed. Not the aspirin, but to go home and pull herself together and stop behaving like an overgrown schoolgirl.

'I'll do the best I can,' she muttered, but before she could move Mark reached out and grasped her hands in his.

'Helen, you're a gem. In fact, if you weren't already married, I'd offer you my hand, my heart and all my worldly goods.'

'A simple thank you would be quite sufficient,' she replied stiffly, pulling her hands free. 'But for the record, don't *ever* ask me to do this again—either of you.'

'She's just kidding,' Tom said uncertainly as his wife strode away, her back ramrod stiff, her head high.

'She looks pretty mad to me,' Mark observed. 'Perhaps I should go after her, tell her to forget it...'

'Helen doesn't mind,' Tom protested with more confidence than he actually felt. 'I'm sure she doesn't.'

'Well, you know your wife better than I do,' Mark said.

Tom stared after his wife. He'd thought he did. Once upon a time he would quite happily have bet money on the fact that he did, but just lately...

'How are you settling into your hospital flat?' he asked, more from a desire to change the subject than from any great desire to know.

Mark shrugged. 'I've been in worse. The main thing I miss is some decent home cooking, but it seems stupid to rent a flat when I'm only going to be here for such a short time.'

'If it's decent home cooking you're after, why don't you come round to our place tonight for dinner?' Tom suggested.

Mark looked tempted, then shook his head. 'I'd better not. It wouldn't be fair to Helen, turning up at such short notice.'

'Don't be daft,' Tom declared. 'Helen will be only too delighted.'

And she would be, he told himself. She'd been in such a funny mood recently, and maybe what she needed was to do something different for a change, and having Mark round for dinner could be just the change she needed.

'Oh, Tom, how *could* you!' Helen exclaimed, banging the oven door shut.

'I thought you'd be pleased,' he said defensively. 'You're always saying we should entertain more, and it must be pretty wretched for Mark, having to go back to an empty flat every evening.'

'But couldn't you at least have invited him for one night next week, given me time to prepare?'

'Mark isn't going to expect any fancy cordon bleu cooking—'

'Then he won't mind if I just open up a couple of cans of beans and shove them on toast?'

A faint flush of angry colour appeared on Tom's cheeks. 'I don't know what you're making all this fuss about. You never bothered when I invited Gideon over for a meal before he and Annie got married.'

'It's not the same,' she protested.

And it wasn't. For a start, Gideon didn't have black hair, and emerald green eyes, and a way of looking at her that sent warm shivers down her back. Gideon didn't make her feel edgy, and confused, and bewildered at the same time.

'Helen…'

'The casserole is never going to stretch to five.'

'Of course it will. You always make too much of everything anyway.'

'It's just as well that I do, then, isn't it? Or we'd all end up having to fill up with biscuits after we've eaten,' she said tartly. 'Tom, I'm not running a restaurant here.'

'What are you fighting about?'

She spun round to see John standing in the kitchen doorway, and bit her lip.

'We're not fighting,' she said as evenly as she could. 'Dinner will be ready in half an hour, so please go and finish your homework.'

'It sounded like you were fighting,' he observed. 'In fact—'

'Mummy and I are not fighting,' Tom interrupted. 'We…we're simply having a discussion.'

'If Emma and I were shouting as loudly as you and Mum were, you'd say we were fighting.'

'Go finish your homework, John.'

They'd spoken in unison, and their son gave them a very hard stare, then trailed away.

'Helen, listen to me—'

'What time did you tell Mark to come round?'

'About eight.'

Oh, brilliant, she thought, really brilliant. Mark would be here in half an hour, and all she had to offer him was a miserable portion of beef casserole and some ice cream and fruit for dessert because it was too late to defrost anything else. And by the time she'd peeled more potatoes and put on extra vegetables, she'd have no time to shower or change her clothes.

'Look, is there anything I can do?' Tom asked.

For a second she was tempted—sorely tempted—to tell him *exactly* what he could do, but instead she said grimly, 'Go tidy the sitting room.'

'I don't know how you do it, Helen.' Mark smiled as he leant back in his seat with a contented sigh. 'Full-time SHO, wife, mother, and after a day like today you can still manage to create a superb meal.'

Tom shot her a look across the kitchen table which said, Told you that you were worrying needlessly, didn't I? Helen got to her feet.

'Emma, John—you've got homework to do.'

'Oh, *Mum!*'

'Now,' she insisted, retrieving their pudding bowls.

'You're not leaving right away, are you, Mark?' Emma asked, sliding reluctantly down from her seat. 'Only you haven't finished telling us about the wombats and koalas—'

'And I want to hear more about the time you went to Ayres Rock,' John chipped in, his grey eyes hopeful. 'Is it really as red as it looks in the pictures? And what about—?'

'Homework,' Tom interrupted firmly. 'Mark isn't going

to run away, you know,' he added as his son and daughter groaned. 'And the quicker you get your homework done, the more time you'll have to badger him before bedtime.'

Mark laughed as the twins shot out of the kitchen. 'You've got a pair of really great kids there. You must be very proud of them.'

I am, Helen thought as she switched on the percolator, but did the children have to make it so obvious they thought he was Mr Wonderful?

Petty, Helen, a little voice whispered at the back of her mind. You're being petty. You're the one who taught them to welcome visitors, so you can't really carp when they do it.

No, but I just wish they hadn't been so clearly charmed by him, she thought as she ran some water into the sink. I wish they hadn't hung on his every word like he was the greatest thing since sliced bread.

'You must let me help with the dishes,' Mark declared, springing to his feet when she reached for the washing-up liquid.

'No, really,' she said quickly. 'I can manage.'

'And we wouldn't feel right, asking a guest to help with the dishes,' Tom said firmly, to her relief. 'I'll show you through to the sitting room—'

'Dad, what do you know about the Aztecs?'

Emma had reappeared at the kitchen door, and Tom frowned.

'As far as I can remember they were one of the earliest of the Mayan people of Central America.'

'But I need to know more than that,' Emma protested. 'I'm supposed to write four hundred words about them for tomorrow.'

'Then why don't you look them up in one of your encyclopaedias?' Helen suggested. 'That's what they're there for.'

'But I've maths to do for tomorrow as well, and

English,' Emma said plaintively. 'Dad, can't you help me? I know I should have started earlier, and I promise I won't ever ask for help again, but couldn't you help me just this once?'

Emma's eyes were huge and beseeching, and Helen shook her head. Emma could always twist Tom round her little finger, and at any other time she might have laughed, but not tonight.

'Emma, it's your homework, not your father's,' she declared, only to see Mark grin.

'Oh, give the kid a break, Helen. Let Tom help her just this once, and I'll help you with the dishes.'

No, Helen thought desperately as Tom gazed at their daughter, clearly torn. Don't go. Please, don't leave me alone with Mark. I don't want to be left alone with him. But to her dismay Tom ruffled their daughter's blonde hair affectionately.

'All right, then, but in future you do your own homework, OK?'

He and Emma were gone before she could protest, and her heart sank as she turned to find Mark smiling at her. That smile which she was beginning to know only too well. That smile which managed to do the oddest things to her heart rate.

'Your daughter's going to be a real heartbreaker when she grows up,' he observed. 'Did you see the way she wrapped Tom round her little finger?'

She lifted some of the plates she'd stacked and thrust them into the soapy water. 'He's too soft with her.'

'Father's usually are with daughters. Not that I've any personal experience, of course.'

'No,' she said dampeningly.

He shot her a quizzical glance. 'She's very like you. The same blonde hair, the same brown eyes.'

'John takes after his father.'

'They're both handsome children but, then, I'd have expected them to be when you're their mother.'

His voice was low, husky, and she took a deep breath, only to immediately wish she hadn't. Tom's aftershave was sharp, tangy, like mountain pine trees, but Mark's was something else. Something sweet, enticing and tantalisingly different. Different enough for her to wonder what it was. Different enough to make her want to lean towards him to inhale it more deeply, so she reached for a dishcloth and began washing the plates as though her life depended on it.

'Helen—'

'You really don't have to help, you know,' she said brightly, too brightly. 'There's not many dishes, and—'

'You know, you're a very attractive woman, Helen.'

Don't do this to me, she thought, staring fixedly at the plate in her hand. Don't flirt with me because I don't know how to flirt—never learned how—and I can't cope with it.

'I'm not attractive,' she replied with a laugh that didn't quite come off. 'Sonia in Paediatrics is attractive. Grace in Men's Surgical is stunning—'

'But I'm not interested in Sonia, or Grace. I'm interested in you.'

He was joking—he *had* to be joking—but as she forced herself to look up, to meet his gaze, she knew that he wasn't, that he meant it, and her heart rate went into overdrive.

'Mark—'

'You're gorgeous, witty, clever—'

'And I'm married, Mark,' she interrupted. 'Married to a man who was your best friend at med school in case you've forgotten.'

'I haven't forgotten,' he murmured, 'but I hadn't realised Tom had branded you with a sign saying, NO COMPILMENTS ALLOWED.'

'He didn't—he hasn't—'

'So why can't I say I find you lovely?'

'Because…because I don't like it,' she floundered, and his eyebrows rose.

'You don't?'

'No, No, I don't,' she said as firmly as she could, and he shook his head.

'You're a lousy liar, Helen.'

'Mark, please…'

'I think you and I could have something very special together. I sensed it the minute I met you, and I know you feel it, too.'

'And I'm *married*,' she exclaimed desperately. 'Tom's my husband, and there's such a thing as fidelity, loyalty, between couples.'

'Not love?'

'Of course, love,' she protested.

'Strange you should mention it third.' He smiled. 'Fidelity, loyalty and then love.'

She stared at him impotently. 'What are you trying to prove—that you're cleverer at word games than I am, smarter? OK, I concede, you're cleverer, but I don't play games—of any kind—and I've had enough of this conversation.'

'Helen—'

'Well, that's the Aztecs taken care of.' Tom smiled as he strode into the kitchen. He came to a halt and glanced curiously from her to Mark. 'Something wrong?'

'Not a thing,' Mark replied smoothly. 'But I think I'll pass on the coffee if you don't mind. I've already taken up more than enough of your time, and I've things to do back at the flat.'

'Nonsense,' Tom protested. 'He can't possibly run away now, can he, Helen? For one thing, the twins will never forgive him.'

She didn't say anything—couldn't—and a hint of a

smile appeared on Mark's lips. 'All right I'll stay, but just for a little while.'

The little while stretched to a full two hours, and by the time he'd gone, and she'd got the twins into bed, Helen had a thumping headache, which wasn't helped by Tom's cheerful chatter.

'Told you everything would be OK, didn't I?' he said as she dragged on her nightshirt, then brushed her teeth. 'All that agonising over the food. Mark's not choosy—never has been.'

'So it seems,' she muttered grimly, pulling back the duvet and getting into bed.

Tom fiddled with the bedside light switch for a few seconds, then sighed. 'Look, I promise I'll give you more warning next time, OK?'

Next time? Over her dead body would there be a next time, she thought, rolling onto her side and tugging the duvet up to her ears.

'The kids really liked him a lot, didn't they?' Tom continued as he slipped into bed beside her. He chuckled as he switched off the bedside light. 'Did you see Emma's face when he was telling her about the alligators—'

'Do we have to talk about this now?' she demanded. 'It's after midnight, and we've got to work tomorrow.'

'Oh. Right. Sorry.'

Tom sounded so contrite that Helen groaned inwardly. It wasn't his fault that his friend was handsome, and charming, and completely amoral. It wasn't his fault that she was bewildered, and confused, and wished she'd never heard the name Mark Lorimer, far less met him.

'No, *I'm* sorry,' she mumbled. 'I shouldn't have snapped at you, but it's been a long day.'

He gathered her to him, spoon-shaped against his chest. 'It's all right, love,' he murmured, nuzzling the back of her neck. 'I shouldn't have sprung Mark on you like that, and I won't do it again without giving you plenty of notice.'

She didn't want plenty of notice. She didn't want Mark in her home ever again.

'Tom, about Mark...' she began, only to come to a halt.

How could she say, Look, your friend's hitting on me? She couldn't. He'd be so angry, and if Mark left the hospital before Rachel returned from her compassionate leave their schedules would be a nightmare. And she shouldn't need to go running to Tom for help. She was a fully grown-up woman who should be able to sort this out herself.

'What about Mark?' Tom asked.

'I was just wondering if he'd ever been married, or in a long-term relationship, or anything,' she lied.

'Good grief, no.' Tom chuckled, his fingers stroking up and down her back, easing the tension there. 'He's a strictly love-'em-and-leave-'em sort of a guy, so I wouldn't recommend introducing him to any of your friends.'

She didn't intend to—especially not to the married ones.

An affair. That's what Mark had been suggesting with all his fancy words and flowery compliments. For them to have an affair.

Well, she didn't do affairs, never had. Some of the staff at the Belfield did. She'd seen it happen on the wards, in the operating theatres, but she'd never been tempted. Never been interested.

Until now.

The words crept into her head before she could stop them, and she bit her lip savagely. What was she thinking? She *loved* Tom. They had a good marriage, two beautiful children, and she could never deceive him, never.

'Tom...' She cleared her throat. 'Tom, have you ever thought—have you ever met another woman—and thought, Wow, but she's terrific?'

'What sort of daft question is that?' he murmured, his hand slipping up under her nightshirt to cup her breast.

'It's not a daft question,' she protested. 'We've been married for ten years, and it would only be natural if you'd found yourself maybe attracted to somebody, maybe tempted to—'

'Sweetheart, you don't half talk a lot of nonsense at times.' He chuckled huskily.

It wasn't nonsense. Surely it was simply human nature to sometimes wonder if the grass might not be greener on the other side? To perhaps occasionally wonder if this was all there was. But how to explain to him, how to say it?

Helen tensed slightly as she felt his fingers slide slowly down her stomach, and when they reached between her legs, rubbing gently at first, then more persistently, she put her hand over his quickly.

'Do you mind if we don't? It's just…it's just that I'm a bit tired tonight.'

The fingers stilled, then withdrew. 'Sorry, love. I should have thought.'

Which made her feel rotten, and guilty, but to make love with him, after what she'd been thinking…

Tom fell asleep quickly. She heard his breathing slow, then deepen, but she couldn't sleep.

Helen lay awake for a long time, staring at the streetlight outside the house, listening to the distant hum of traffic from Great Western Road, and wished with all her heart that she'd never met a man with a shock of black hair and a pair of sparkling green eyes.

CHAPTER FOUR

'You're going to be just fine, Rhona,' Helen insisted as the woman stared nervously up at her from the theatre trolley. 'The anaesthetist will be here in a minute to give you an injection, then all you'll have to do is sleep.'

'I know,' Rhona said, then swallowed convulsively. 'It's just... Thanks for coming down with me, Doctor, for staying with me until I go in. I really appreciate it.'

'It's no trouble.' Helen smiled.

Which wasn't strictly true. In fact, hanging about outside the operating room, waiting for the anaesthetist to arrive, was scarcely the most productive use of her time, but Rhona had been so clearly terrified when the porter had arrived to collect her from the ward that coming down with her had seemed the only thing to do.

'It's the waiting I can't stand,' Rhona continued, her head turning anxiously as the door opened and one of the theatre nurses appeared. 'I just wish they'd get on with it.'

'It won't be long now,' Helen said soothingly. 'I understand Dr Brooke and Dr Lorimer have almost finished scrubbing up—'

'Dr Lorimer's nice, isn't he? And he has a way of talking to you... Well, you just know you can trust him, don't you?'

Oh, really? Helen thought sourly. She wouldn't trust him as far as she could throw him, and that wasn't very far. She might have been shaken and confused when Mark had come to dinner on Thursday, but she wasn't confused now. She was angry.

Just who the hell did he think he was? Offering her a cheap, sordid affair, and expecting her to be flattered. And that's what he'd been offering, she'd no doubts about that. All his fancy talk about them having something special together— He'd meant an affair, but she wasn't some bimbo with half a brain cell and no pride. She was worth more than that—a hell of a lot more than that—and he could stuff his flattery and his compliments where the sun didn't shine.

'This operation that Dr Lorimer is going to do on my Fallopian tube,' Rhona continued. 'It's quite a difficult one, isn't it?'

'It's Dr Brooke who's performing the surgery—Dr Lorimer is simply assisting,' Helen replied as evenly as she could, 'and it's difficult because the instruments he'll be using are so tiny.'

'Couldn't he just use ordinary instruments—make it easier for himself?'

Helen smiled. 'How big do you think your Fallopian tubes are, Rhona?'

The woman frowned. 'I've never really given them much thought. Something like a garden hose, perhaps?'

The theatre sister choked and Helen laughed, too. 'Rhona, at its thinnest point your Fallopian tube is about the size of a piece of button thread.'

'Cripes,' the woman gasped. 'I knew Dr Lorimer was good, but I didn't realise he was that good.'

Helen gritted her teeth. 'It isn't Dr Lorimer who's performing the surgery, it's—'

'OK, we're ready to roll,' Mark declared, coming through the swing doors of the theatre looking for all the world as though he'd just stepped off the set of some glossy American medical drama. 'Time for you to go to sleep, Rhona.'

She managed a wobbly smile. 'If you say so, Doctor.'

'Hey, stop worrying,' he said, his green eyes smiling at her from above his mask. 'I haven't lost a patient yet.'

'Thanks for coming down, Helen,' Tom muttered in an

undertone as the anaesthetist inserted a needle into the back of Rhona's hand and asked her to start counting. 'I understand she was in a bit of a state.'

'I didn't mind,' she replied. 'I just hope everything goes OK, and you don't find anything else wrong.'

'I'm sure we won't,' Mark said, overhearing her. 'And thanks for your help, Helen. Like Tom said, we appreciate it.'

To Tom's surprise his wife coloured, muttered something unintelligible under her breath, then strode through the waiting-room door, letting it clatter shut behind her. Which wasn't like her, but, then—just lately—there'd been a lot about his wife that wasn't like her.

Like the animosity she obviously felt towards Mark. If he even mentioned his name her face became rigid, and yet the dinner on Thursday had gone really well. The kids had certainly enjoyed it. They were already asking when Mark would be coming back.

'Helen's excellent with patients, isn't she?' Mark commented as the theatre nurses wheeled a now unconscious Rhona into the operating theatre.

'She could have made a first-rate surgeon, too,' Tom replied absently.

'Really?' Mark exclaimed.

'Vital signs perfect—ready to go whenever you are,' the anaesthetist observed.

Quickly Tom made an incision into Rhona's abdomen to accommodate both the microscope and instruments, then gently slid the microscope into her uterus.

'Helen won the gold medal for surgery in her final year at med school.'

'You're kidding?' Mark said, and Tom shook his head.

'Straight up, no kidding.'

'Then why on earth is she still an SHO? If I'd won a gold medal—'

'Emma and John came along rather sooner than we'd planned, so…'

'She put her career on hold to look after them,' Mark finished for him. 'You're a lucky man, Tom. Not many women would have been prepared to do that.'

He *was* lucky, Tom realised guiltily, especially when he couldn't actually remember ever sitting down with Helen and discussing which of their careers would take a back seat until the children were older. Somehow it had just sort of happened that she'd stayed home to look after the twins until they'd been old enough to go to nursery, and she hadn't appeared to resent it. At least she'd never said she had.

Maybe she did now. Maybe that was what so many of her recent odd conversations had been about. The ones she'd start, then shake her head and mutter something about it being not important, for him to forget it.

Perhaps she was trying to work up the courage to tell him she wanted to leave the Belfield, to try for a promotion at a different hospital.

What was it she'd said to Mark about them still being there ten years after they'd qualified?

'Who's to say what's round the corner for any of us—what changes we might make?'

Did she mean she wanted to leave? If she did, then they'd leave. She'd given up so much for him over the years that there was no way he was going to stand in her way for something she really wanted.

'How does it look?' Mark asked when the microscope was in place.

'Right Fallopian tube completely blocked, as we suspected,' Tom replied, 'but luckily the blockage doesn't seem to extend through the wall of the uterus into the uterine cavity. Want to see for yourself?'

Mark did.

'It looks like a straightforward cut, remove and sew-up job to me,' he observed.

'Oxygen reading normal, BP steady, everything A-OK here,' the anaesthetist announced.

Tom flexed his shoulders. 'OK, let's go for it.'

It was a long operation, and a delicate one. Removing the damaged part of the Fallopian tube was difficult enough, but what was equally important was to ensure no damage was caused to any of the surrounding delicate structures. A careless scrape here—the very slightest abrasion there—would cause adhesions to form, and then the whole operation would have been pointless.

'You're wasted here, mate,' Mark said in obvious admiration when Tom finally straightened up after inserting the last tiny stitch into Rhona's rejoined Fallopian tube. 'With your skill you could make a fortune if you went abroad.'

'Maybe.'

'Maybe nothing,' Mark insisted. 'You'd have a queue of infertility clinics lining up to employ you if you put the word out that you were available.'

Tom smiled as he checked Rhona's uterus for signs of excessive bleeding, then waited while the tiny instruments he'd used were counted by the theatre nurses. 'I wouldn't want to do fertility treatment all the time. I enjoy the variety of Obs and Gynae too much.'

'Then why don't you apply for an Obs and Gynae post abroad?' Mark asked as he took Tom's place at the operating table and began stitching the incision he'd made into Rhona's stomach. 'Why struggle on here with substandard equipment and not enough staff?'

'Because I like it. It's a good hospital, Mark, despite its shortcomings,' he continued as Mark shook his head. 'And Gideon's working on Admin, trying to get them to agree to us having another member of staff.'

'Yes, but—'

'What we really want is our own infertility clinic. A clinic affiliated with Obs and Gynae, but with its own consultant, rather than us doing both the infertility and our normal work. Gideon thinks Annie's brother, David, might be interested if we can get it up and running. He's working as a specialist registrar at the Merkland Memorial at the moment, but he's not happy there and I think he'd come to us like a shot if we could offer him a consultancy.'

'*If* being the salient word,' Mark said when Rhona was wheeled, still unconscious, into the recovery room where the nurses would monitor her breathing, consciousness and blood pressure as she emerged from the anaesthesia. 'You're an idiot, Tom—you know that, don't you?'

'Some of us would call him loyal,' one of the theatre nurses declared tightly, clearly having overheard their conversation, and Mark grinned.

'Well, somebody obviously agrees with you.'

Tom wondered if Helen did. Did she think he was loyal, or did she think he was a fool? It was time he found out.

Helen wasn't thinking about loyalty, or the hospital, or her future. She was too busy trying to keep her temper.

'It was Dr Brooke who performed your Caesarean, Mary,' she declared tersely once Mrs Alexander had come to the end of her eulogy of how wonderful Mark Lorimer was, how skilled, how handsome. 'He was the one who delivered your baby, made sure nothing went wrong during the operation.'

'I know, but Dr Lorimer's so kind, so thoughtful, isn't he, and have you noticed his eyes, Doctor? They're green.'

I don't care if they're sky-blue pink, Helen longed to yell at her. Yes, he's handsome, yes, he's a good surgeon, but he's only been here three weeks. My husband's worked at the Belfield for ten years, and he's a considerably better surgeon, but just because he's not jaw-droppingly handsome, and doesn't trot around flattering everybody, he's suddenly become invisible.

'Did Dr Brooke explain that we'll be keeping you and your baby in for about a week?' she asked as calmly as she could.

Mary nodded. 'He said I've to keep taking the heparin when I go home.'

'Only for about six weeks,' Helen reassured her. 'It's just to make sure the clot has completely gone.'

'I know. Dr Lorimer came to see me yesterday, and he explained all about it. He gives you such confidence, doesn't he—Dr Lorimer?'

Helen counted to ten, and managed a very small, tight smile. 'I'm just pleased everything's turned out all right for you,' she said, before turning abruptly on her heel and walking out of the ward.

'You look fit for murder,' Annie declared when Helen swung into the staffroom and yanked a cup out of the cupboard. 'Anybody I know?'

'Let's just say I'm getting a little bit tired of all our patients assuming that the only surgeon we have in Obs and Gynae is Mark Lorimer,' Helen replied grimly. 'And if that sounds petty, I'm sorry but right now I *feel* petty.'

Annie chuckled. 'Don't apologise to me. Personally I'm beginning to wonder if I should start carrying a sign saying, REMEMBER MY HUSBAND? HE'S ACTUALLY THE CONSULTANT IN CHARGE OF THIS DEPARTMENT.'

'What is *wrong* with everybody around here?' Helen continued, banging the cup down on the staffroom table, then following it with the jar of coffee. 'Are they all cracked?'

'I don't know about everybody, but that coffee jar and mug are certainly in serious danger.'

The junior doctor's eyes were brimming with laughter, and Helen groaned. 'I'm going crazy, aren't I? I've totally lost the plot, and I'm going crazy.'

'I think you just don't like your husband being ignored any more than I like my husband being sidelined,' Annie observed as Helen spooned some coffee into the mug. 'The trouble is, Mark looks so very much the part, doesn't he?'

'Looks aren't everything,' Helen retorted. 'It's brains and ability that count, not black hair, green eyes, and a tan. It's skill and dedication that are important, not whether you can chat up every woman in sight. And not just chat them up, but hit on them, suggest that they—'

She came to a horrified, panic-stricken halt. She'd said too much—way too much. There was concern in Annie's eyes, and not just concern, and if she didn't start back-tracking fast she was going to be asked questions she most certainly didn't want to answer.

'I'm sorry,' she continued quickly with a laugh that sounded false even to her own ears. 'I'm overreacting—I know I am—but I'm sick to death of all this "isn't Mark wonderful" stuff.'

'And all the attention he's been giving you.'

It wasn't a question, it was a statement, and hot colour flooded Helen's cheeks. 'I haven't been encouraging him.'

'Men like Mark Lorimer don't need encouragement,' Annie sighed. 'In fact, I think they positively thrive on *dis*couragement.'

'Annie—'

'Helen, I'm not prying, and I know it's none of my business, but I've seen the way he looks at you—the way you look at him—and...' The junior doctor shook her head. 'Jamie's father was the same—handsome, charming and... Look, I guess what I'm trying to say is be careful.'

How could the girl know—how could she possibly know what Mark had said on Thursday night? She couldn't. There was no way she could.

'I'm sure I don't know what you mean,' she said as evenly as her thudding heart would allow. 'Mark... He's just a colleague, and even if he wasn't, I'm married. *Happily* married.'

It was Annie's turn to redden. 'I didn't mean that you— I wasn't suggesting that you would ever, but— Helen, I'm sorry. I shouldn't have said anything, and I'm sorry.'

Not half as sorry as I am, Helen groaned silently as Annie made her excuses and shot out of the staffroom. If Annie had noticed Mark was paying her a lot of attention, did that mean other people had seen it, too? They couldn't have, or surely she would have noticed the sly looks, the winks and nudges, and she hadn't seen anything. At least, not yet.

Angrily she took a sip of her coffee. The quicker Mark Lorimer left the Belfield the better, but he'd only been here three weeks. Three weeks—another three to go. She'd be lucky if she got through them without killing him.

Or falling into his arms, a little voice whispered, and she shook her head vehemently.

'Never,' she muttered out loud. *'Never.'*

'It's the first signs, you know—talking to yourself.'

She glanced round to see Tom smiling at her, and managed a small smile in return. 'If that's the case, I should have been committed years ago. How's Rhona?'

'Good. The blockage hadn't extended into her uterus, so we cut and rejoined.' He sank down into the chair beside her, his eyes weary. 'Only time will tell if the op's been successful, but I hope it is. I really don't want to tell her that her only hope of getting pregnant is through IVF.'

Helen nodded. So many women thought IVF was the quick and easy answer to their infertility problems, but in reality it could often turn out to be a devastating disappointment.

'Do you want a coffee?' she asked, seeing him rotate his neck, clearly trying to ease the tension there.

'I could murder one,' he admitted. 'It was a long op,

though it would have been even longer if Mark hadn't been there to help me.'

'It's about time he pulled his weight,' she muttered under her breath as she switched on the kettle, but Tom heard her.

'Look, what is it with you and Mark?' he demanded. 'Ever since he arrived you've been antagonistic towards him, and it's so unfair. He didn't have to fill in for Rachel. He could have swanned around Europe before going to Canada, instead of helping us out. He's a great bloke, Helen. Everybody likes him—'

'I didn't realise it was compulsory to become a member of the Mark Lorimer fan club,' she retorted, and he thrust his fingers through his hair impatiently.

'There you go again—being snide, snippy. He's a good doctor, and he likes you—I know he does—so couldn't you at least *try* to be a little friendlier towards him?'

Was he out of his mind? No, of course he wasn't. Tom was honest, and decent, and it would never occur to him for a second that his friend might be showing more than a purely friendly interest in his wife.

Then tell him, her mind argued. Tell him what Mark said. What he implied, suggested.

But she couldn't. She'd only ever seen Tom in a blazing temper once, and that had been when the twins had been three, and a young man had sideswiped their car when he'd overtaken them. Tom had dragged the young man out of his car, and for one awful, dreadful moment she'd thought he might actually kill him. No, she couldn't tell Tom what Mark had said, and awkwardly she held out a cup of coffee to him.

'I just… I don't like his attitude. He's too casual, too laid back.'

'You mean he flirts too much. Oh, come on, Helen. It's harmless. It would be different if he was harassing somebody.' She flushed despite all her best efforts not to, and his eyes shot to hers, weary no longer. 'He's not, is he? Look, if he's bothering somebody at the hospital…'

'Of course he's not,' she said quickly, fighting down her mounting colour. 'I think—I suppose—I've just sort of got used to working with just you, Gideon, Annie and Rachel. Mark does things differently, that's all.'

'You're sure that's all?' he demanded.

Oh, Lord, she hated lying to him, but lying was better than the truth, infinitely better. 'Of course I'm sure,' she declared.

For a second she thought he was going to question her further, but to her relief he didn't. Instead, he took a sip of his coffee, then said something that threw her even more.

'Helen, you know when the children were born—how you put your career on hold to look after them. Did you resent it?'

She stared at him in confusion. 'Why on earth would I have resented it? They're our children, and I wanted to look after them.'

'Yes, but did you ever think, Why can't Tom do the looking after, why does it have to me whose career gets shelved?'

She thought back to when they'd brought the children home from the hospital. How tiny they'd been, how very vulnerable.

'No, I never thought that. It's probably very old-fashioned of me, and anti-feminist or something, but I just thought that as I was their mum I should stay home with them.'

'But now they're older,' he pressed. 'Would you like to get your career back on track—maybe start applying for some specialist registrar posts? I'll support you all the way if that's what you want,' he continued, as she gazed at him, even more bewildered. 'If you've heard of a job at a different hospital, don't let any worries about me stand in your way. I'll just up sticks and follow you.'

'But I thought you liked working here at the Belfield?' she said.

'We're not talking about me, we're talking about you, and as Mark said—'

'Mark said what?' she interrupted, her voice ice-cold.

He looked uncomfortable. 'He just happened to mention how much you'd given up for me.'

'Oh, he did, did he?' she snapped. 'Well, Mark Lorimer knows nothing about me, and what I want.'

'But he's got a point.'

'I don't care if he's got a million points,' she flared. 'He has no right to interfere in our lives.'

Tom shook his head impatiently. 'He wasn't interfering. He just happened to point out what I should have been aware of myself.'

She all but ground her teeth.

'Tom, listen to me, and listen good. The day I live my life according to what Mark Lorimer thinks I should do is the day you can have me committed!'

Or gagged, she thought with a groan when she heard the sound of a throat being cleared and turned to see the man himself standing in the doorway of the staffroom.

How much had Mark heard? Too much, from the way his eyes were gleaming, and she didn't know whose cheeks were redder—hers or Tom's.

'Something I can help you with?' Tom said tightly.

'Gideon would like a word if you've got a minute.'

Tom didn't reply. He simply strode out of the staffroom, leaving Helen gazing unhappily after him, and Mark cleared his throat again.

'I'm sorry about that. Walking in on a disagreement, I mean.'

He didn't look sorry. He didn't look one bit sorry, and she headed for the door, only to have him block her way.

'Helen, how long are you going to keep running away from me?'

She met his gaze with a cold, hard stare. 'I am not running away. I simply have work to do, so if you'd stand aside, please?'

He didn't. 'You're running, Helen. Running from what you and I could have together.'

She didn't let her gaze slip—wouldn't allow it to, even though his eyes were making her heart do those unwelcome and uncomfortable back flips again. 'You have a good opinion of yourself, don't you?'

'I'm just being honest, and you're not. I've never met anybody like you—'

'Then you should get out more.'

'Helen…' He reached out and touched her cheek, and she jumped back as though she'd been stung.

'Don't do that!'

'Why?' he demanded. 'If you don't feel anything for me, why should you care if I touch you?'

His voice was rough, uneven. Hers didn't sound any steadier when she whispered, 'Stop it, Mark. Please…please, stop it. I'm married—'

'You keep saying that,' he said irritably. 'Like it was a life sentence or something. Marriages should only last when they're fun, not because they've become a comfortable routine.'

'My marriage isn't like that,' she retorted.

'No? Then when was the last time you and Tom made love?'

Crimson colour darkened her cheeks. 'I don't think that's any of your business.'

'I think it is. I think it's very much my business if your marriage is over, and you're just hanging in there out of habit.'

'Mark—'

'Think about it, Helen. Think long and hard.'

He'd gone before she could think of anything cutting to say, and she desperately wanted to think of something cutting. Wanted to chop him down to size, to make him see once and for all that his attentions were as unwelcome as he was.

Hell's bells, it shouldn't be that hard to do, she told herself as she walked along to the ward, all too aware that her legs were none too steady. If it was anybody else hassling her like this, she'd be able to do it in a minute.

And that was the trouble, she realised as she pushed open the door of Obs and Gynae. It wasn't anybody else. It was Mark Lorimer and, try as she might to deny it, she was attracted to him. He made her feel feminine, and attractive, and if she hadn't been married…

But you *are* married, she reminded herself. You're married, and you love Tom, even if he does irritate the hell out of you at times. Good grief, you probably irritate Tom, too, but that doesn't mean you don't love each other, so get a grip, woman, and pull yourself together.

Rhona Scott didn't want to pull herself together. She wanted to apologise for having fallen apart earlier.

'You must think I'm such a wimp, Doctor,' she murmured unhappily when Helen stopped by her bed. 'Needing you to hold my hand before I went into the theatre.'

'Of course I don't think you're a wimp,' Helen insisted. 'Everybody's nervous before they have an operation.'

'It wasn't just the operation. I just don't like hospitals. The needles, the smells, being surrounded by ill people…' Rhona bit her lip. 'That sounds awful, doesn't it? Awful, and dumb.'

'You'd be surprised to learn how many people feel the same.' Helen smiled. 'I hated being in hospital myself when I had my twins.'

'But you're a doctor,' Rhona protested. 'You can't have been frightened.'

'Don't you believe it,' Helen said, her eyes dancing. 'Doctors make the worst patients of all. We know too much, you see. So stop feeling guilty and embarrassed. You've got nothing to apologise for.'

But I do, she thought as she noticed Tom going into Liz's small office. I've been so crabby and crotchety with him, and it's not his fault. OK, so maybe I've felt taken for granted, but I'm not blameless either.

I change into a pair of tatty old jeans and a sweatshirt when I get home from work because I can't be bothered to do anything else. I slump in front of the TV with the kids after dinner, then go to bed and sleep because it's too much effort to do anything else.

Mark said that marriages worked only when they were fun, but he was wrong. Marriages worked when you worked at them. When you made an effort for each other no matter how tired you felt. And she hadn't been making any more effort than Tom had.

Well, it was time for a change, and as she caught sight of herself in the ward mirror she knew exactly what the first change was going to be.

Her hair.

For the past ten years she'd kept it shoulder length because it was easy to manage, but she had an appointment this evening at the hairdresser's for her usual six-weekly trim, and she was going to tell Jason she wanted something different. Something different, and pretty, and sexy.

'Everything OK, Helen?' Annie asked as she hurried by in answer to Liz's call.

'Not yet, Annie.' Helen smiled. 'But after tonight…after tonight, it's going to be.'

'Wow,' Helen's daily help exclaimed when she finally arrived home that evening carrying two shopping bags. 'You look sensational, Doctor.'

'Jason at the Rainbow Salon said he thought I'd suit it

shorter, feathered into a cap,' Helen replied, her hand going self-consciously up to her hair. 'He's put in some gold highlights, too, and I'm not a hundred per cent certain about them, or the style.'

'Has Dr Brooke seen you yet?'

Helen shook her head, and it felt odd to have no ponytail bouncing on her shoulders, no hair escaping from a scrunchy. 'He's not due home for another half-hour. My hair—you really think it looks OK?'

'Doctor, when your husband gets home I guarantee he won't be able to keep his hands off you.'

Helen chuckled, and blushed. That's what she was hoping, but she'd taken out some extra insurance just in case. In one of her carrier bags was everything she needed to make Tom's favourite meal of steak, mushrooms and salad, and in the other bag was a scarlet—and quite indecently sheer—nightdress she'd bought on impulse from the lingerie shop on the corner of Byres Road.

'Where are the children?' she asked, quickly slipping the steak under the grill.

'In the sitting room, watching TV.'

They watched too much TV. Normally, she'd have gone in as soon as her daily left and told them to get up to their bedrooms and make a start on their homework, but not tonight. Tonight she wanted a little time to herself.

Time to investigate the contents of her wardrobe, and sigh over the singularly uninspiring selection that met her gaze.

'Shopping,' she told herself as she pulled out the pale blue blouse Tom had given her last Christmas and the soft tartan skirt she'd bought two years ago and had never worn. 'It's high time you went shopping.'

And then you'd better sign yourself into the psychiatric unit and get your head examined, she thought with a shaky laugh as she pulled on the blouse and skirt, because you're actually following all the suggestions in those dreadful articles in women's magazines. The ones entitled 'Ten Ways to Rekindle the Desire in Your Man's Heart'.

But, Lord, she did look different, she thought when she stood back to examine herself in the dressing-table mirror. Younger, she thought, and totally, totally different.

Emma and John clearly thought she looked different, too, when she went into the sitting room and switched off the TV.

'I didn't know you were going out,' her daughter said, her brown eyes critical.

Yikes, but that shows when I last made an effort in the evening, Helen thought ruefully. 'I'm not going out. I just thought I'd put these on as I haven't worn them before.'

Emma digested that for a second, then obviously decided it wasn't worth pursuing. 'You've had your hair cut.'

'And?' Helen prompted.

'It's OK.'

She supposed that was child-speak for a big improvement. She hoped it was.

'What do you think, John?' she asked, turning to her son.

He shrugged. 'Yeah, you look OK.'

Which wasn't exactly the most fulsome of praise either but, then, they were just children, Helen reminded herself as she ushered them up to their bedrooms and went back to the kitchen. It was Tom's opinion that mattered. Tom who she wanted to say, Wow, Helen, but you look stunning.

'Mum, Dad's home!' Emma yelled down from her bedroom.

She'd already heard the car. Would he come into the kitchen, or go straight through to the sitting room?

The sitting room. He'd be tired—probably want to sit down, put his feet up.

Well, he wouldn't be tired or angry soon, she thought with a secret smile.

A quick check of the grill revealed the steak was done to perfection, and she headed for the sitting room to find her husband sifting impatiently through the comics strewn on the sofa.

'Helen, where's the morning paper?' he demanded. 'Gideon said there's an article in it on foetal distress syndrome—'

'It's on the coffee-table.'

Nervousness made her voice sound deeper, huskier than usual, and he must have heard it because he glanced over his shoulder, then straightened up slowly and stared at her. 'You…you've had your hair cut.'

Did he mean he liked it, or he didn't? She couldn't tell.

'What do you think?' she asked, turning round so he could see the back. 'I thought I'd go for a new look.'

'It's…different.'

Different? Where was the 'Wow' and the 'Helen, you look stunning' she'd been expecting? 'Different' didn't come close—not anywhere near close.

'You don't like it,' she said, feeling a quite ridiculous impulse to burst into tears.

'I didn't say that,' he declared quickly. 'It's…nice.'

'Nice' wasn't any better than 'different'.

'In other words, you don't like it,' she exclaimed, and he gazed at her with exasperation.

'I *do* like it. I just said so, didn't I?'

'No, you didn't. You said it was nice, different.'

'Well, there you go, then.'

'That doesn't mean you like it.'

'Of course it does. Hell's bells, Helen…' He came to a halt, and sniffed. 'Is something burning?'

The steak. Oh, Lord, she'd forgotten all about the steak, and with a cry of alarm she raced to the kitchen, pulled the grill out of the oven, only to cough and splutter as a pall of black smoke belched out.

'Cripes, what on earth was that before it was inciner-ated?' Tom asked, throwing open the window.

'Steak,' she muttered. 'I cooked steak for your dinner.'

He stared down at the charred remains. 'It doesn't mat-ter. I'm not that hungry anyway. Soup will do me fine, and then I think I might have an early night. I'm bushed.'

Soup. He wanted soup when she'd been going to give him steak. He wanted sleep when she'd been going to put on the sexy nightdress she'd bought. He didn't like her new hairstyle, and he hadn't even noticed she was wearing the blouse he'd bought her for Christmas.

Well, he could have his soup, she thought, choking down the hot tears she could feel welling up into her eyes as she heard him returning to the sitting room. He could have his early night, too.

In fact, as far as she was concerned, he could have as many early nights from now on as he wanted.

CHAPTER FIVE

'THERE you go, Jennifer—two happy, eighteen-week-old foetuses bouncing around in your tummy like mini-athletes,' Tom commented, pointing to the shadowy shapes on the monitor. 'Would you like to know what sex they are?'

Jennifer craned her neck to stare at the screen. 'I'd rather it came as a surprise, if you don't mind. They—the babies—they are all right, aren't they?'

'Perfect,' he reassured her. 'I just wish I knew why your blood pressure was so high. It was up last month when my wife tested you, and it's still up today. What have you been doing?'

'Nothing, Doctor, honestly,' Jennifer insisted. 'There's no way I'd do anything to endanger my babies.'

He knew she wouldn't—not after having previously undergone three unsuccessful IVF treatments—but something was causing her BP to climb, and he needed to know what.

'Any headaches, visual disturbances, swollen ankles?'

Jennifer shook her head. She also looked worried. 'Is something wrong? Doctor, I couldn't bear it if I lost them. To have got this far… If I lost them now…'

Quickly Tom came round the examination trolley and clasped her hands in his. 'Jennifer, I'm going to do everything in my power to ensure these babies go to full term.'

'I know, but…' Tears filled her eyes. 'You're not a magician, are you?'

'No, but I've been known to work wonders,' he declared, his lips curving. 'In fact…' He came to a halt as the department secretary appeared and discreetly put a piece of paper down on his desk. 'Ah, good. This looks like your blood and urine test results. Maybe they'll give us some answers.'

They didn't. Jennifer's sugar levels were as normal as they'd been when Helen had tested her a month ago, and so were her blood platelets.

'Frankly, I don't care how much my blood pressure goes up,' Jennifer said when Tom told her. 'All I'm bothered about is my babies.'

Tom wished it was as simple as that as he reached for his appointment book. The possibility of pre-eclampsia was what was worrying him, but he had no intention of sharing his concern with Jennifer. She'd been through enough already.

'I'd like to see you again on the 13th of May.'

'So soon? But—'

'It's nothing to worry about,' Tom lied, seeing Jennifer's surprise. 'We doctors are just never happier than when we're performing tests.'

'The 13th—that's a Friday, isn't it?' She laughed a little nervously. 'Unlucky for some.'

'Look, if you're superstitious we could make it the day before.'

'It's all right—the Friday will be fine. Will I see you or Dr Helen?'

'Me, unless I'm unexpectedly called away.'

Jennifer nodded, and Tom stared at her thoughtfully. 'Would you prefer to see my wife? I can arrange it, if you like.'

'Could you? It's not that I don't have every confidence in you, Dr Brooke,' Jennifer continued in a rush. 'It's just that Dr Helen... She's a woman, and a mother of twins herself, and—'

'You'd like to see her if it's at all possible. It's OK, Jennifer,' he said gently. 'I'm not offended. I'll check with my wife and see if she can book you in for the 13th, but if not you'll see me, OK?'

Jennifer look relieved. 'I saw Dr Helen in the corridor before I came in. She looks stunning with her new haircut, doesn't she?'

Tom's smile became fixed. 'Yes. Yes, she does.'

'It really changes her appearance. Makes her look totally different.'

It did, Tom thought as he showed Jennifer Norton out. It made her look like a stranger. A beautiful, unknown stranger. A beautiful, *remote* stranger, he amended with a sigh when he sat back down again at his desk. A stranger who was in a huff.

She had been in a huff ever since last week when she'd got her hair cut—and he couldn't for the life of him think why. Dammit, he'd said she looked nice, and yet when he'd said it she'd looked as though she'd been about to burst into tears.

Perhaps 'nice' had been the wrong word to use, but he'd been so bowled over when he'd seen her. She'd looked so beautiful, so very, very beautiful. Maybe he should have told her that instead. Or then again perhaps not, considering what her reaction had been when Mark had said she looked gorgeous. Lord, but the look she'd given him had been positively glacial.

So if 'nice' wasn't enough, and 'gorgeous' was too much, what the hell *had* she wanted him to say?

With a sigh he hit his intercom button. 'Could you send in my next patient, please?'

'That's all of them, Dr Brooke,' the department secretary replied.

He glanced at the small pile of files in his in-tray. 'Are you sure, Doris? I've still got some folders here—'

'They're all no-shows, Doctor.'

He gritted his teeth. He hated it when that happened. If a woman had to cancel because of family illness or some other problem, it was understandable, but to just not bother to turn up… It was the height of selfishness, for one thing.

Some other woman could have had the appointment, and their waiting list would have been that much shorter.

'Looks like you'll get a proper lunch today, Doctor,' the secretary continued.

A proper lunch. He couldn't remember the last time he'd had a proper lunch at work. A sandwich or a packet of crisps was all he usually managed, but today he could actually have a lunch. It sounded good. It sounded wonderful.

And if he was *really* lucky Helen might be free, too, he thought as he headed for the door. They could have lunch together. A nice leisurely lunch, just the two of them, without Emma and John bickering as they usually did at mealtimes. A nice leisurely lunch during which he and Helen could talk, and maybe he'd find out what he'd said or done that had so obviously upset her.

'I'm sorry, but I can't,' Helen said when he found her on the ward. 'I promised Liz I'd help her with the inventory of the drugs cupboard.'

'I'll do it for you, Helen,' Annie said, overhearing her. 'You go and have a nice lunch with Tom.'

'But I thought you were on your way down to the canteen yourself?' Helen protested, and Annie shook her head.

'I've changed my mind. I've been putting on a bit of weight recently, so it's time I started counting the calories.'

'But—'

'I believe the canteen's serving lasagna today,' Tom murmured, his eyes fixed on his wife. 'Unfortunately I can't promise you that anyone will sing "O sole mio", or that there'll be strawberries and chocolate mousse for pudding, but...'

Helen's lips curved into the first genuine smile he'd seen all week. 'Maybe that's just as well,' she said.

He shook his head, his eyes warm. 'Oh, I don't know. It would certainly give everybody something to talk about, wouldn't it?'

Annie was staring at them blankly, but Helen knew what he was talking about. He could tell from the faint blush of colour on her cheeks that she was remembering, as he did, the *pensione* off St Mark's Square in Venice where they'd spent their honeymoon.

Every night, without fail, the owner had served them lasagna, followed by strawberries and chocolate mousse. Every night he'd serenaded them with the same song, as they'd sat, their hands entwined, oblivious to anything but each other. And every evening after dinner they'd gone up to their small bedroom with the squeaky bedstead and made love.

'What do you say, Helen?' he pressed softly. 'Is it a date?'

'Well, if Annie doesn't mind helping Liz,' she began, 'I think—'

'Ah, Tom, the very man I've been looking for,' Gideon exclaimed as he strode towards them. 'I've got the operating schedule worked out for next week so could you come and cast your eye over it, see if you'd like any alterations or amendments?'

So much for the lasagna, Tom thought wistfully. So much for the quiet lunch with Helen. Annie obviously thought so, too, because she said vexedly, 'Gideon, does Tom really have to check the schedule right now? He and Helen were just going down to the canteen to have lunch.'

'Sorry about that,' her husband replied, 'but I'm operating all afternoon, and if I don't get the list in quickly we'll end up fighting for theatre space with the other departments.'

There was nothing Tom could say. He knew their work always took priority, but he couldn't help but think as he accompanied Gideon along to his consulting room that he'd have been a lot happier if it hadn't been Annie, but Helen, who'd looked so disappointed at the cancelled lunch.

He'd thought—hoped—that reminding her of their honeymoon might make her forgive him for whatever he'd said or done, and it had seemed to be working until Gideon had arrived with his damn theatre schedule. The moment the list had been mentioned all the softness in her face had disappeared, and she'd walked away without a word.

Words weren't the problem with the list Gideon had prepared. Concentrating on them was, and his abstraction must have been all too apparent because eventually Gideon put down his sheet of paper and said, 'OK, what's wrong?'

'Wrong?' Tom repeated blankly.

'You're a million miles away, and it's not like you, so what's the problem?'

For a second Tom chewed his lip, then sighed. 'Do you understand women, Gideon?'

'I don't think any bloke ever does—not really,' the consultant replied. 'Oh, as a medical man I might know what bit goes where, what bit does what, but as to what makes them tick—I haven't a clue.'

'Neither have I,' Tom said with feeling, and Gideon leant back in his seat, his expression thoughtful.

'So Annie was right. I told her she was imagining it, but she said she thought you and Helen might have had a row.'

How did women do it? Tom wondered. He would have sworn only he could tell that Helen was being distinctly cool towards him, but Annie had sensed it, realised it.

'It's not so much that we've had a row,' he began uncomfortably. 'It's just that she's been in a huff with me ever since she got her hair cut last week.'

'You told her you liked it, didn't you?'

'Of course I did,' Tom protested defensively. 'I distinctly remember saying it was different, and nice, and since then—major huff.'

Gideon frowned as he slipped the theatre schedule into

a folder. 'Maybe you should talk to Mark. He's supposed to be the expert on women, isn't he?'

He was, but there was no way Tom was going to ask Mark for advice. Talking to Gideon was one thing, but Mark… He didn't know why, but he most definitely didn't want to talk to Mark about Helen.

'I expect it will work itself out,' he said quickly. 'Helen doesn't usually stay in a huff long.'

'Have you been paying her enough attention recently?'

A slow burn of heat crept up the back of Tom's neck. Oh, hell, if Gideon was asking about his love life then he was out of here. Admitting that Helen was in a huff was one thing, but admitting that he hadn't made love to his wife in ages was something else.

The consultant would want to know why, and the last thing he intended confessing was that either he was usually too tired or Helen was. Gideon would probably say that was a poor excuse, and he had a horrible suspicion he'd be right.

He tugged uncomfortably at his collar. 'I…um…'

'The only reason I'm asking is because Annie buys all these women's magazines, and they're always full of letters from women complaining about husbands and boyfriends not paying them enough attention. Maybe you need to take Helen out to dinner or the cinema or something?'

Tom let out his breath in a slow sigh of relief. Taking Helen out to dinner was something he was prepared to discuss, not least because it would give him the opportunity to point out how impossible it was at the moment.

'You know what our shifts are like, Gideon. If I'm not at the hospital, Helen is, and if she's not at the hospital, I am.'

'How about buying her some flowers, then?' Gideon suggested. 'Annie loves getting little posies of pansies or freesias.'

'Pansies don't seem like much of a peace offering,' Tom said uncertainly, and to his surprise the consultant flushed.

'Well, it works for Annie, but you know your wife better than I do.'

Mark had said that, too, Tom remembered when Gideon headed for the operating theatre, but did he—did he really?

It had been Mark who'd pointed out how much she'd given up when the children were born. Mark who'd reminded him of what a very good surgeon Helen had been at med school. OK, so when he'd tackled her about it she'd said she'd never regretted her decision, but maybe she'd just said that to please him. Or, then again, maybe she'd been telling the truth and Mark had been as wrong as he was.

He swore under his breath. Why couldn't women be as uncomplicated as men? Why couldn't they come right out and *say* whatever was bugging them instead of going off in a huff?

A door clattered open behind him and he saw Doris elbowing her way out of her office, heavily weighed down with files.

'Here, let me help you with those, Doris,' he exclaimed, walking quickly towards her and relieving her of more than half of her bundle before she could protest. 'Are you taking them up to Admin?'

'They want them a.s.a.p. apparently,' she said breathlessly, pushing back the lock of grey hair which had escaped from her bun. 'Honestly, the amount of time this hospital spends on files and forms. I bet if we dumped half of them, not only would nobody not even notice but you and Mr Caldwell could probably fit in another ten operations a week.'

'Probably,' he agreed.

'Did you manage to have a nice lunch, Dr Brooke?' she continued as they walked together towards the lift.

'I'm afraid something came up, and it was a packet of crisps again.'

She shook her head at him. 'Honestly, you doctors. You spend all day lecturing your patients about the importance of a good diet, and yet you're the worst offenders when it comes to food.'

She had a point, Tom thought wryly. She could also, he suddenly realised with a flash of inspiration, be the answer to his problem.

There was no way he could take Helen out to dinner, couldn't even buy her flowers when he was working until late all week, but Doris could buy them. She could slip out to the florist this afternoon, buy Helen a nice bouquet and he'd give them to her tonight. Helen would be happy, he'd be happy and everything would be back to normal again.

The doors of the lift swung open as they reached it and he turned to Doris with what he hoped was his best and most appealing smile.

'Doris, I need you to do me a favour.'

'I still think it's a shame you and Tom didn't get a chance to have lunch together.'

Helen tightened her grip on her stethoscope. If Annie had said that once this afternoon, she'd said it three times, and it was really beginning to get on her nerves.

'It's no big deal, Annie,' she said tersely. 'It's not like we were going somewhere special like Stephano's or anything.'

'No, but—'

'Mrs Scott's husband will be here soon to collect her, Helen,' Liz interrupted, 'and I understand you want a word with her before she leaves?'

Helen nodded. Tom had taken out Rhona's stitches yesterday, then given her the rundown on what she should and shouldn't do after her tubal surgery, but he hadn't felt

a hundred per cent certain that the woman had taken it all
in, so she'd offered to speak to her before she left.

'Helen—'

'You'll have to excuse me, Annie.'

'I just wanted to say that if you and Tom ever *did* want
to go somewhere special,' Annie said quickly, 'maybe out
for a meal or something, Gideon and I would be only too
happy to babysit for you.'

'That's very kind of you,' Helen said in surprise, 'but I
couldn't possibly impose.'

'You wouldn't be imposing—we'd love to do it. Look,
will you at least think about it?' Annie urged as Helen
opened her mouth to protest. 'The offer's there, and at least
at somewhere like Stephano's there wouldn't be any
chance of Gideon popping up in the middle of your meal
wanting Tom to check out theatre schedules.'

There wouldn't be, Helen thought with a smile as she
made her way towards Rhona Scott's bed, but unfortunately the likelihood of both her and Tom having the same
evening off any time in the near future was as probable as
Admin agreeing to them having an additional member of
staff.

Still, Annie had meant her offer kindly.

Or because she can't stand the atmosphere between you
and Tom any longer, her mind pointed out, and her smile
faded.

Annie obviously knew something was wrong. All these
efforts she was making to get her and Tom alone together.
Volunteering to help Liz with the inventory, offering to
babysit the children. She must have been reading the same
magazine article she had, and she wondered if she should
tell Annie it was a waste of time.

Being in a huff wasn't exactly working either, she
thought with a deep sigh. In fact, being in a huff was
distinctly childish and immature.

So why don't you make the first move? her mind suggested. Apologise, say you're sorry.

Why should I apologise? she argued back. *I'm* not the one who's stupid and blind. I'm not the one who's got about as much romance in my soul as a block of wood, so why *should* I apologise? It's up to Tom to say something first, not me, and if that's childish, too, then so be it.

Rhona Scott wasn't being childish and immature, but something was clearly worrying her as she packed her suitcase, and it didn't take Helen long to find out what.

'Dr Brooke's already warned me about not lifting anything too heavy or getting constipated,' she replied when Helen repeated Tom's instructions. 'He also said that if I wasn't pregnant by Christmas he'd think about recommending IVF treatment.'

'And you're not happy about that,' Helen observed, seeing the woman sigh. 'Look, I know you have a phobia about hospitals, and IVF treatment involves spending a lot of time in one—'

'It's not that, Doctor. It's…' Rhona sat down on the edge of her bed. 'I want to start the IVF treatment right away. I'll be thirty-seven in June, and to wait until Christmas… Why can't I start the IVF treatment sooner?'

'Because now that Dr Brooke has cut out the blocked sections of one Fallopian tube you've a sixty per cent chance of becoming pregnant without assistance. Rhona, no matter what the newspapers say, IVF isn't the answer to every woman's prayer,' Helen continued as the woman looked unconvinced. 'The success rates are still very low—no more than one in six—whereas now you have a three out of five chance of doing it naturally.'

Rhona didn't look happy, and Helen shook her head as she watched her leave. How many times had she heard women demand IVF as though it was the quick-fix answer to everything? She wished it was, but all too often it brought nothing but pain and heartbreak.

'A penny for them?'

She turned to see Mark standing behind her, and sighed.

'I'm just thinking of all the women in the world who want babies and yet can't have them, and all the babies who are born to women who don't want them.'

'And then there are people like Mr and Mrs Dukakis,' he said. 'I had to tell them this morning that they're both carriers of the thalassaemia gene, so the odds are stacked pretty high that their baby will have the condition.'

'How did they take it?'

His mouth twisted. 'How do you think?'

He looked tired, defeated—nothing like his usual smiling flippant self—and instinctively she put her hand on his arm.

'We can only do what we can, Mark.'

'I know, but…' He rubbed his hand over his face. 'Do you ever wish you had a magic wand which would erase all the illnesses and inherited conditions in the world?'

'I think every doctor does,' she replied, 'but when I get down—wonder why the hell I'm doing this job—I think of all the lives modern medicine has saved, the lives it will go on saving as new treatments become available, and then I think maybe the magic wand isn't too far away.'

His lips twisted into not quite a smile. 'I've said it before, and I'm going to say it again. Tom is one very lucky man. I mean it, Helen,' he continued as she backed up a step, her cheeks darkening. 'Straight up, no flattery, no bullshit.'

'I'm lucky, too,' she said quickly. 'Tom's a good husband—'

'Do you want to hear something really crazy?' he interrupted. 'I *like* you, Helen Brooke, and that's a whole new experience for me. Oh, I know all about *wanting* a woman, but liking one?' He looked bewildered, then a broad grin lit up his face and he looked like the old Mark again. 'Said it was crazy, didn't I?'

She didn't know what to say—couldn't think of anything *to* say.

Did he realise how devastating his admission was? No, she didn't think he did. He hadn't said it for effect or as another form of flattery. He'd meant it, and somehow—crazily—his confession was infinitely more appealing than all his previous compliments had been, and much more dangerous.

'Mark—'

'I'd like to take you out to dinner one evening.'

'I'm afraid Tom and I hardly ever get the same night off,' she replied, and he smiled.

'Don't be disingenuous, Helen. You know very well that I wasn't including Tom in my invitation. It's *you* I want to take out to dinner.'

She shook her head. 'I can't.'

'Why not?'

'You know very well why not,' she protested.

'Look, all I'm talking about is dinner here,' he continued, his green eyes fixed on her. 'Dinner in any smart restaurant you care to name. Dinner in a restaurant that would cut up rough if I dragged you under the table halfway through the hors d'oeuvres and main course and made love to you. A simple dinner for two.'

Who was being disingenuous now? she thought. They could never go out together for a simple dinner for two. If she accepted his invitation she'd also be accepting—acknowledging—the attraction between them, and that was something she must never do.

'No, Mark.'

'Trying to pretend that what's happening between us isn't really happening isn't going to work, you know,' he said softly.

'Mark…' She paused, and started again. 'Mark, I—'

'Mark, you're needed down in A and E,' Liz called from her small office. 'RTA. Female passenger, five months pregnant with chest and leg injuries.'

He sighed. 'No rest for the weary.'

No, but a reprieve for me, Helen thought as she watched him go, and she badly needed that reprieve. Needed time to think. No, not to think, she told herself. Thinking about Mark Lorimer and what he'd said would be a mistake, a big one.

Home, Helen thought, catching sight of the time on the ward clock. She needed to go home, to the children, to everything she and Tom had created, and remind herself of what was important in her life.

One hour at home, however, was enough to make her wonder about her decision. Two hours had her questioning her sanity.

'Do you two never do anything but fight?' she exclaimed as she went into the sitting room in time to see Emma hurl a book at her brother.

'He started it,' Emma protested. 'He's always in my way, mucking about with my things.'

'I wouldn't touch your rubbishy old things with a bargepole,' her brother retorted. 'You're just mad at me because you got into trouble at school today, and I got three gold stars.'

'What sort of trouble?' Helen demanded.

'Nothing,' Emma replied, shooting her brother a fulminating glance.

'Emma, what sort of trouble?' Helen repeated.

'She was fooling about in class again,' John declared, looking as smug as only an eight-year-old-boy could, 'so the teacher sent her to the headmistress.'

'That's right, go telling tales to Mum,' Emma snapped. 'You're a big jerk, and I hate you.'

And to think I gave up the chance of becoming a surgeon for this, Helen thought wearily as John responded in kind. I should have gone on the Pill instead of trusting to Tom and his condoms. Better yet, I should have got myself sterilised.

'Why were you fooling about in class?' she asked as evenly as she could.

'It was boring.'

'That's it?' Helen said. 'It was boring? Well, let me tell you something, young lady. A lot of life is boring, but you've got to take the rough with the smooth. It can't all be—'

'Fun, fun, fun,' Emma finished for her. 'Yeah, I know. I should do. You keep telling me.'

Helen opened her mouth, closed it again and gave up an argument she knew she couldn't win. 'Bedtime,' she said instead.

'Oh, *Mum*!'

For once her son and daughter were united, but she was adamant.

'Bed,' she repeated. 'It's way past nine, and your father won't be pleased if he comes home and finds the two of you still up.'

Actually, Tom probably wouldn't even notice, but she needed some peace and quiet. Now.

And time to try to salvage some of his dinner. The chicken casserole was still OK, but the vegetables were a total write-off.

Should she put more on now, or wait until Tom got home?

Now, she decided, slipping some roasted potatoes onto a tray and the broccoli into a pot. He'd be starving by the time he got home, and as she was on call tonight it would be just typical if the hospital paged her just as he walked in the door.

'Something smells good.'

She whirled round, her hand on her heart. 'Tom, are you trying to give me a heart attack!'

'I'm sorry,' he said ruefully. 'I was trying to be as quiet as I could so as not to wake the kids.'

'They've just gone up.' Her eyes swept over him, taking in the greyness round his jaw, his tired eyes. 'Rough shift?'

He lifted the cruet set on the kitchen table, and put it down again. 'Did you hear about the RTA—five-month pregnant woman with chest and leg injuries?'

She nodded. 'Mark was on his way down to it when I left.'

'She didn't make it. Neither did the baby.'

There was nothing she could say—nothing that would make it any better. They'd both had experiences like that in the past, but it never got any easier to handle.

'Why don't you go and sit down?' she suggested. 'Dinner won't be long.' Quickly she salted the broccoli, put the lid on the pan and reached for her oven gloves, only to see he hadn't moved. 'Is there something else?'

He disappeared into the hall and reappeared clutching the biggest bouquet of flowers she'd ever seen. 'These…these are for you.'

'For me?' she faltered. 'But—'

'I thought…well, you've seemed a bit down lately,' he said awkwardly, 'and I thought they might cheer you up.'

A hard lump clogged her throat as she took the flowers from him. He'd bought flowers for her when it wasn't her birthday. He'd found time in the middle of his fraught, awful shift to go out and buy flowers for her.

'They're lovely,' she said a little unsteadily. 'Thank you.'

'You're sure you like them—I mean, they're all right?'

Oh, Lord, but he looked so uncertain, and she blinked back the tears she knew were shimmering in her eyes. 'They're beautiful. You shouldn't have—'

'Of course I should,' he protested. 'I don't buy you

flowers often enough. I don't buy you anything often enough. I should buy you flowers, and chocolates, and perfume—'

'Tom, you don't need to buy me anything to prove you love me,' she said through a throat so tight it hurt. 'Just…just maybe tell me once in a while that you do.'

'Then they're all right?' he said, relief coursing through him. 'You really do like them?'

'Oh, Tom, you big ninny,' she said with a queer little laugh that sounded almost like a sob as she came round the table into his arms. 'Of course I like them.'

And he gathered her to him, and did what he'd been wanting to do all day, captured her lips with his own, revelling in the taste of her, the feel of her soft warmth under his hands, the pressure of her breasts against his chest.

Lord, but it had been so long since they'd made love. Too long, he realised, feeling his groin tighten in anticipation as she moaned against his mouth when he slid his fingers up under her blouse, searching for, and finding, the catch of her bra. Much, much too long, he decided with a groan of frustration when she suddenly pulled back from him just as his fingers cupped her bared breasts.

'Tom, we can't,' she said breathlessly. 'I'm on call tonight. The phone could ring at any minute.'

'Maybe it won't,' he said, coaxing her back into his arms, kissing the silky soft hollow in the centre of her throat where he knew she liked to be kissed. 'Maybe we'll get lucky.'

'Fat chance,' she said with an unsteady laugh. 'And you haven't eaten yet. You must be starving.'

'I sure am,' he murmured huskily, encircling one of her nipples with his fingers and smiling as she gave a gasp of pleasure. 'But not for food.'

'At least let me turn off the oven,' she said, her eyes

dark and soft and luminous. 'And put your lovely flowers into some water.'

Impatiently he watched as she switched off the cooker, but when she lifted the flowers he couldn't help but say, 'I'm so glad you like them. I wasn't sure what Doris would buy—everyone's taste's different—and—'

'Doris,' she repeated, with an odd expression on her face. 'You asked Doris to buy them for me?'

'I'd much rather have bought them for you myself, of course,' he said hastily, 'but I'm so busy at the moment—'

'Too busy even to lift the phone, and at least order them personally?' she snapped. 'Nobody's that busy, Tom.'

'Helen—'

'So you asked Doris to buy them for me,' she continued furiously. 'Doris, who's the biggest gossip in the hospital. Doris, who'll know it isn't my birthday, or our anniversary, so she'll guess we've had a row.'

'She won't—'

'Was it her suggestion to buy them for me?'

'No, of course it wasn't. It was—' Quickly he choked off the rest of what he'd been about to say, but not quickly enough.

'It was who, Tom?' she said, her voice icy. 'Who suggested buying me flowers?'

'Gideon,' he muttered, 'but—'

'So, not content with discussing our private life with Doris, you told Gideon as well. Well, thanks, Tom. Thanks for nothing!'

'Helen—'

'I'm going to bed.'

'But—'

'I'm going to bed, and you know what you can do with your damn flowers!'

She'd slammed out of the kitchen before he could stop her, and for a moment he wondered if he should go after her, but something told him that if he were to suggest making love now he'd probably end up sleeping in the spare room.

Morosely he stared down at the flowers left abandoned on the kitchen table. They were nice flowers—they were beautiful flowers—and she'd loved them. He knew she had, until…

'Women,' he muttered out loud to the empty kitchen. 'If I live to be a hundred, I don't think I'll ever understand women.'

CHAPTER SIX

'HELEN, the very person I'm looking for!'

Helen's heart sank as she turned to see Gideon coming towards her, a broad smile on his face.

He was going to ask about the flowers. The flowers Tom had given her last night and she'd binned this morning. And she didn't want to talk about them. Not today. Not ever.

'I'm in a bit of a hurry, Gideon.'

'Aren't we all?' He beamed. 'But I'd like a word with you before I see Tom.'

Of course he would. He was clearly itching to know how successful his idea had been. To find out how pleased she'd been with the flowers. And she *had* been pleased until she'd discovered who'd bought them, whose idea they'd been in the first place.

'Gideon—'

'It's such good news, Helen, such tremendous news. And it's going to make such a difference to our lives.'

She stared at him blankly. Good news—tremendous news? What on earth was he talking about?

'I'm not making any sense, am I?' He laughed, seeing her confusion. 'But I've just come from a meeting with Admin, and they've finally agreed to us advertising for another member of staff. And not just any old member of staff, but a consultant. A consultant who'll be in charge of a newly created infertility clinic affiliated to Obs and Gynae.'

'You're joking?' she gasped, and he shook his head.

'I've got permission to start working on the advertisement this morning.'

'But that means...'

'No more fifteen-hour days.' He nodded. 'No more one weekend off in four, and, best of all, our own infertility clinic.'

'Oh, Gideon...'

'It sounds wonderful, doesn't it?' He laughed. 'And I wanted you to be the first to know. You've been working so hard recently.'

'We all have.'

'Yes, but you're a wife and mother as well as our SHO, and I know things haven't been easy for you recently.'

A faint wash of colour crept over her cheeks. How much had Tom told him? At a guess, not a lot. Men didn't discuss their feelings with other men the same way women did, but Gideon clearly knew—or at least suspected—enough to be concerned.

'Gideon—'

'I'm not going to say any more,' he continued quickly, obviously wishing now that he hadn't actually said anything at all, 'except that I'm sure that once you and Tom can spend more time together everything will be all right again.'

She hoped it would as Gideon hurried off to spread the good news, but could the problems she and Tom seemed to have be fixed simply by spending more time with each other?

All marriages have their rough moments, her heart whispered. That's what the 'for better, for worse' part of the wedding ceremony is all about. You work through the difficult times, and come out stronger on the other side. And marriages don't break up because of a bunch of flowers. Women don't start thinking about the big D word simply because they feel neglected, taken for granted. OK, so maybe right now Tom appears to have as much sensitivity as a hospital trolley, but you love him, and he loves you.

'I was beginning to think you'd got lost,' Liz said when Helen reached the ward.

'Gideon wanted a word,' Helen replied with an effort. 'Any new admissions this morning?'

'A Mrs Yvonne Merrick. She's one of Tom's patients, but I think you saw her last month when you took over his clinic. Mother of four—vaginal bleeding between her periods?'

Helen nodded. She remembered Mrs Merrick very well. The poor woman had been terrified that she might have cervical cancer, and unfortunately her smear had come back from the lab showing abnormal cells.

'She's scheduled for a cone biopsy on Thursday, isn't she?' Helen asked.

Liz nodded. 'We've also got in a sterilisation, a D and C and a pelvic-floor repair job.'

Helen took the notes the sister was holding out to her. 'Anything else I should know?'

'Yup, but you're not going to like it.'

Liz's eyes were gleaming, and Helen shook her head. 'I'm afraid I'm not up to guessing games this morning, Liz. Just tell me, OK?'

'Your favourite patient was readmitted last night.'

'My favourite patient?' Helen repeated, only to groan when she followed Liz's pointed gaze. 'Mrs Foster's *back?*'

'Apparently she developed severe stomach pains last night after she'd finished wallpapering her sitting room.'

'After she did *what?*' Helen gasped.

'Hey, this is Mrs Foster we're talking about, remember,' Liz said. 'The woman who burst her hysterectomy stitches while trying to go to the loo.'

'Yes, but—'

'Her husband said she's very house-proud.'

'Did her husband also say she was an idiot?' Helen protested, then frowned when a thought suddenly occurred to her. 'Just a minute. You said she was admitted last night?'

'That's right.'

'But I was on call last night, and nobody phoned me. Who admitted her?'

Liz flicked through the notes left by the night staff, then shook her head. 'That can't be right. It says here that Mark did, but—'

'He wasn't on call last night—I was,' Helen completed for her.

'Do you want me to find him, ask what happened?' Liz asked, and Helen shook her head.

'I'll speak to him later. What damage has Mrs Foster done?'

'Mark wasn't sure, according to these notes, so he's booked her in for investigative surgery on Thursday.'

Which was going to completely wreck their operating schedule, Helen thought, fuming inwardly, and it was all so unnecessary. A hysterectomy wasn't some trivial procedure, the operational equivalent of slapping a plaster on a cut finger. It was major surgery, surgery that took both time and great skill to perform, and yet because of her own stupidity Mrs Foster could have endangered all the work Tom had done.

'How is she this morning?' she asked, her face tight, angry.

'Not happy.'

It was the understatement of the year. Far from being chastened and upset, Mrs Foster was in full complaining mode. If her operation had been carried out by a better surgeon this wouldn't have happened. If the facilities at the Belfield weren't so inferior she wouldn't have had to be brought back in again.

'Does that woman possess no working brain cells?' Helen demanded when she finally managed to make her escape. 'Everything that's happened is her own damn fault, and yet to hear her talk you'd think we were the ones to blame.'

'A classic case of too much money and not enough to do, if you want my opinion,' Liz replied. 'Which isn't something either you or I will ever suffer from.'

Too true, Helen thought ruefully, only to stiffen when she saw Tom coming into the ward.

He looked tired. Tired and drained, as though he hadn't slept last night. She hadn't slept either, perched on the very edge of their mattress, deliberately maintaining a wide, cold space between them, and it hadn't been any better when they'd got up.

They'd eaten a virtually silent breakfast together, a silence broken only by Emma's and John's chatter, and then they'd shared an equally silent drive into work. Occasionally she'd felt his eyes on her. Had once even heard what had sounded suspiciously like an impatient huff, but determinedly she'd said nothing.

Petty, Helen, her heart whispered as she stared at her husband. Giving him the silent treatment is petty. Does it matter who suggested buying you flowers—who actually bought them? Tom must have been really worried about you to talk to Gideon, so what does it matter whose idea they were?

'Doris said Tom bought you some flowers yesterday,' Liz said. 'Is he in the doghouse for something, or have the two of you got something to celebrate?'

Yes, it does damn well matter, Helen thought grimly, her guilt evaporating in a second under the speculative gleam in Liz's eyes. *She* wasn't the one who might just as well have told the world and his wife that they'd had a row. *She* wasn't the one who'd admitted—actually *admitted*—that the flowers hadn't even been his own idea in the first place, and had then got Doris to buy them for him.

'Tom just wanted to buy me some flowers, OK?' she retorted. 'It's nothing to get excited about.'

And that was stupid, really stupid, she thought, groaning inwardly when she saw the sister's eyebrows rise.

Why hadn't she made a joke about it? Said, What husband isn't in the doghouse at some time or another? Being defensive hadn't got her anywhere. Being defensive had simply fanned the rumour mill that Doris had already started, judging by the curiosity on Liz's face.

'Liz—'

'I hear Mrs Foster's been readmitted,' Tom interrupted as he joined them. 'What happened?'

Never did Helen think she'd actually welcome the opportunity to talk about their most troublesome patient, but she welcomed it now. The woman might be a complete pain in the butt, but at least she was a safer topic of conversation than those damn flowers.

'It seems she developed severe stomach pains last night after she'd finished wallpapering her sitting room,' she replied.

'After she finished doing *what*?' he exclaimed, and Helen nodded.

'I know, but apparently Mrs Foster's very house-proud.'

'Mrs Foster would also appear to be in dire need of a brain transplant,' Tom declared grimly, then frowned. 'Just a minute. You said she was admitted last night? But you were on call last night, and I didn't hear the phone ring.'

Both of them would have heard the proverbial pin drop in the stony silence that had hung over their bedroom last night, she thought uncomfortably, but she didn't say that.

'I can only think that somehow the switchboard must have called Mark by mistake,' she said instead.

'The switchboard isn't paid to make mistakes,' he flared. 'Mark worked a fifteen-hour shift yesterday, and the last thing he needed was to be called out during the night.'

'I know, but—'

'Why didn't he tell them you were on call, not him?'

'I don't know,' she protested, noticing out of the corner

of her eye that Liz was tiptoeing discreetly away. She didn't blame her. She didn't much like being interrogated first thing in the morning either. 'Look, the switchboard made a mistake, and for some reason or another Mark decided to take the call. End of story.'

'No, it isn't,' he insisted. 'We're all entitled to time off. Would you like to be called out in the middle of the night if you were off duty?'

'Of course I wouldn't,' she said, 'but I don't know why they called him and not me. If you're so concerned about it, why don't you ask Mark or the switchboard?'

'There's no need to get snippy.'

'I am not getting snippy,' she hissed, uncomfortably aware that his voice was rising and Annie was watching them curiously from the end of the ward. 'It's you who's making a big deal out of this.'

'That's right—blame me,' he retorted. 'Everything seems to be my fault nowadays, so blame me.'

Why was this happening? Helen wondered as she stared up into her husband's stormy face. Why did they appear to be totally incapable of having any sort of conversation nowadays without riling one another?

'Tom—'

'I wish to heaven I'd never bought you those damn flowers.'

'You didn't, as I recall,' she flashed back before she could stop herself, then bit her lip when his eyes rolled heavenwards. 'Tom, I'm—'

'Look, are you going to beat me over the head with those damn flowers for ever?' he asked. 'I'm sorry, OK? I shouldn't have asked Doris to buy them for you, OK? What more do you want from me?'

For you to tell me you love me, she thought, her heart twisting inside her. I just…I want you to tell me you love me. I want you to say that you find me desirable, and attractive, and I mean more to you than just a cook, a housekeeper and the mother of your children.

Tears burned in her throat. Desperate, unhappy tears. 'Tom…Tom, do you love me?'

He stared at her as though she'd just said something completely ridiculous. 'Helen, this is hardly the place—'

'Tom, do you love me?' she insisted.

'Of course I do,' he replied, impatience and irritation plain on his face. 'Good grief, we've been married for ten years, haven't we?'

It wasn't an answer. Not the answer she wanted, and certainly not the one she needed.

'Tom, please—'

'I have to go,' he interrupted as his pager went off. 'Look, we'll talk about this some other time—later—tonight.'

They wouldn't, she thought as he hurried away. He was working until eight o'clock this evening, and the eight o'clock would probably become nine or ten, and by the time he got home he'd be too tired to discuss anything, or she'd be called out, and so it would go on, and on.

Mark had said marriages ended when they were no longer fun, but what happened to a marriage when you felt you no longer knew your husband? When you didn't know what he thought, or how he felt? OK, so she'd always known Tom found it difficult to put his feelings into words but how hard could it be for him simply to tell her he loved her?

Unless he didn't.

The thought sliced through her brain like a laser.

Maybe he didn't love her any more. Maybe that was what all their rows and arguments were about. He didn't love her any more, and their marriage was over.

How often had she heard the words 'I didn't know—I never suspected that he was having an affair' from distraught female friends? How often had she supplied the tissues and the comforting shoulder, and thought how lucky she was? It had never occurred to her, not for a minute, that her own marriage might end not with a bang, but with a whimper. End because of irritation, or boredom, or familiarity.

'Helen, I don't like to hurry you but it's way past ten, and your ward round should have started half an hour ago.'

I don't care if it's past midnight, Helen thought, turning blindly to see Liz hovering behind her. I don't care if I never do another ward round in my life. My marriage is falling apart. I think my marriage is falling apart, and I want to find Tom to ask him, to find out, but I can't. I'm an SHO. I have a job to do, and I've got to do it, even if it feels as though my whole world is collapsing around me.

Somehow she got through the morning. Somehow she managed to reassure the D and C patient, and the sterilisation one, and even managed to smile a farewell to Mary Alexander, who was finally going home with her daughter.

'I'm just so very grateful to everybody.' Mary beamed. 'You've all been so marvellous.'

'Just don't forget to keep taking the heparin,' Helen reminded her. 'We don't want you back in again with another clot.'

And Mary smiled, and nodded, and she and her husband were so happy, so obviously very happy.

Yvonne Merrick wasn't. Yvonne was frightened, and tearful, and clearly wanted to be anywhere but here.

'Has Dr Brooke explained what's going to happen on Thursday?' Helen asked, sitting down on the edge of her bed. 'That he's going to remove a piece of your cervix under a general anaesthetic?'

'He said he would test the sample, and if…if it proved to be cancerous he would use a laser to burn the cells out.'

'You're not going to feel anything, Yvonne,' Helen said, seeing the way the woman was twisting and untwisting the bedcover between her fingers. 'The procedure's completely painless—'

'But what if the sample reveals cancer?' Yvonne whispered. 'My aunt—she had cervical cancer years ago, and when they operated they found it had spread everywhere. What if—?'

'Yvonne, we'll cross that bridge when—and if—we get to it,' Helen said firmly, but Yvonne wasn't listening.

'I should have gone to my GP about the bleeding—I know I should—but I kept hoping it would go away.'

How often had Helen heard that? Too often. But there was no point in telling Mrs Merrick she'd been stupid. The woman obviously already knew it.

'Look, why don't you try to get some rest?' she said instead. 'Or if you can't,' she continued, seeing Yvonne shake her head, 'why not go through to the television room? Worrying about what might or might not happen on Thursday isn't going to do you any good.'

Neither is worrying about the state of my marriage, Helen thought as she walked slowly out of the ward and along to the staffroom. If Tom has decided it's over, then I want to know, for him to tell me so.

'You look as rough as I feel,' Annie said when she saw her.

'I've certainly had better mornings,' Helen admitted. 'Is there any tea left in that pot?'

'Whatever's left will be well and truly stewed,' the girl said, getting to her feet. 'I'll make you some fresh.'

'There's no need.'

'It's no bother,' Annie declared, emptying out the used teabags and switching on the kettle. 'I tell you one thing, Helen, the sooner this new consultant arrives, the better. It must be five or six weeks since Gideon and I managed to get a weekend off together.'

Helen couldn't remember the last time she and Tom had been off together. Maybe that was the trouble. Maybe they'd simply drifted apart. But if they had, surely they could get together again?

'Isn't happy at the Merkland Memorial.'

Oh, Lord, what was Annie talking about? Something about the Merkland Memorial. Her brother David worked there, didn't he?

'You think your brother might be interested in the post here?' she hazarded, hoping she was right.

'Oh, he'll be interested all right, but Gideon wants the best man for the job. I, of course, think David would be far and away the best, but...' Annie shook her head, and laughed. 'I could just be the teeniest little bit biased.'

Helen smiled as she took the cup of tea the junior doctor was holding out to her. 'It's no bad thing to be biased in favour of somebody you love.'

Slowly she unwrapped the sandwiches she'd bought from the canteen, only to frown down at them. Ham and pickle. Why on earth had she bought ham and pickle? It was Tom's favourite, not hers. With a sigh she took an unenthusiastic bite, then glanced up to see Annie's eyes on her.

Lord, had Annie just asked her something? Get your brain in gear, Helen. Get your brain in gear, and pay attention.

'I'm sorry, but my mind was miles away,' she said with an uncertain laugh. 'What did you just say?'

'Nothing, actually, but... Look, I don't want you to think I'm being nosy or anything, but Doris said Tom bought you the most gorgeous flowers yesterday.'

Was there anybody in the hospital who didn't know about those damn flowers? If there was, she wanted to shake that person by the hand.

'Annie—'

'I just love getting flowers, don't you?' the junior doctor continued brightly. 'They make you feel so special, so cared for.'

I've got to tell somebody, Helen thought. If I don't tell somebody I'm going to go mad, and Annie's not a gossip, I know she's not.

'Not if the person who gives you the flowers didn't actually buy them,' she sighed. 'Not if it wasn't even their idea in the first place, but somebody else's.'

'Sorry?' Annie said in confusion.

'Tom didn't buy me the flowers, Annie. He asked Doris to buy them for me, and it was Gideon who came up with the idea.'

'Did Gideon tell you that?' the junior doctor demanded. 'If he did, I'm going to kill him when he gets home tonight.'

'No, it wasn't Gideon,' Helen replied with an uneven laugh. 'It was Tom.'

'Tom *told* you that he didn't buy the flowers, and they were Gideon's idea?' Annie shook her head and muttered something unprintable under her breath. 'Lord, but men can be such idiots.'

'And uncaring,' Helen murmured, but Annie heard her.

'No, not uncaring,' she said quickly. 'It's obvious that Tom loves you—'

'Is it?' Helen interrupted with a crooked smile. 'I'm afraid I'm beginning to wonder about that.'

'Oh, Helen…'

Annie didn't get a chance to finish what she'd been about to say. The door of the staffroom swung open and Mark appeared.

'Hey, would you rather I went back out again?' he said, his eyebrows rising quizzically as Annie bit her lip with annoyance and Helen gazed at her sandwich as though it was the most riveting thing she'd ever seen. 'If I'm interrupting something…'

'Of course you're not,' Helen said with an effort. 'We were just discussing the new consultant—wondering who it will be.'

'Do you think Tom will apply for the post?' he asked, pulling up a chair, and sitting down as the staffroom phone rang and Annie went to answer it. 'I know he likes his Obs and Gynae work, but it would be a big step up for him.'

How should I know? Helen thought. I don't know anything about what goes on in my husband's head any more.

'That was X-Ray for me,' Annie said as she put down the phone. She glanced uncertainly from Mark to Helen. 'It's not urgent, so if you'd rather I stayed…?'

Helen shook her head. 'Don't be silly. I'm fine.'

'You're sure?'

'Of course I'm sure,' she said firmly, but Mark clearly didn't think she was as Annie left. He was gazing at her thoughtfully, and her heart sank. Could he have heard about the flowers, too? Stupid question. Of course he had, and the last thing she wanted was to discuss her husband with him. Think, Helen, she told herself, think, and then she remembered. 'What's this I hear about you moonlighting for me?'

'Moonlighting?' he repeated, as he extracted a packet of crisps from his pocket. 'I'm sorry, but—'

'I understand you admitted Mrs Foster last night.'

To her surprise he suddenly looked very uncomfortable. Uncomfortable, and not a little embarrassed. 'The switchboard got through to me by mistake.'

'Then why didn't you simply tell them I was on call, not you?' Good Lord, was he *blushing*? No, of course he wasn't. He probably hadn't blushed since he was knee high to a grasshopper, but he certainly looked rather red. 'Mark—'

'When the switchboard said it was Mrs Foster, I guessed you wouldn't exactly be thrilled to see her,' he muttered, 'and…well, I thought you looked kind of tired when you left yesterday, and you've got your kids to look after and everything, and...' He shrugged. 'Look, it was no big deal.'

But it was, she thought as she stared at him. He'd thought she looked tired so he'd taken the call for her. He'd noticed she was out of sorts so he'd volunteered to see Mrs Foster even though he must have been exhausted himself. It was what a caring husband would have done—or a lover.

'I'm very grateful,' she said awkwardly, and he smiled, a smile that sent a shiver racing down her spine.

'Any time, Helen.'

So much meaning in two little words. So much promised, implied, suggested. Her mouth felt dry, tight, and she ran her tongue over her lips quickly, and saw something deep and enticing flare in his eyes.

'Mark, I...' Her heart was thudding so hard it was difficult to breathe, far less speak. 'Mark...'

He was holding her hand. She couldn't for the life of her remember how he'd got hold of it, but his thumb was tracing a gentle pattern on the sensitive skin on the inside of her wrist. Up and down, circling, caressing, teasing, sending shivers racing down her spine, pooling deep down in her stomach, and she swallowed, hard.

He was going to kiss her. She knew instinctively that he was going to kiss her. Did she want him to?

No.

Yes.

She didn't know.

'Relax, Helen,' he murmured. 'Let it happen.'

And she did. Traitorously her head tilted sideways as he lowered his lips to hers. Even more traitorously her lips parted so his tongue could delve deep inside her mouth, and it was intoxicating, and enticing, and wrong.

This is *wrong*, her heart cried as she felt herself responding, yielding to the excitement of his lips. This is so *wrong*, she thought, hearing herself give a tiny groan as his hands slid up her sides to cup her breasts. Desperately she jerked away, her heart racing, her cheeks scarlet.

'Helen—'

'No,' she said, seeing the confusion in his eyes, knowing it was mirrored in her own. 'You shouldn't—we shouldn't—'

'If I don't kill Mrs Foster in the next twenty-four hours, it'll be a miracle!' Tom exclaimed as he slammed open the staffroom door. 'Ye gods, *she* was the one who was wallpapering. *She* was the one who put her hysterectomy at risk, and yet whose fault is it she's back? Mine, of course!'

'W-would you like a coffee, Tom—or some tea?' Helen said, getting jerkily to her feet, willing her legs to work.

'Tea would be great. Hey, is that a spare ham and pickle sandwich?' he added, his eyes lighting up.

She mumbled something in reply but it could have been anything. All she could think was that not only had she let Mark kiss her, she'd kissed him back. How could she have done that—*how?*

Tea, she told herself, forcing her feet towards the teapot. Pour Tom out some tea. Pull yourself together, and pour him out some tea, and pray—*pray*—that he doesn't notice how much your hands are shaking when you give it to him, how flushed your cheeks must be.

He didn't. He was too busy explaining to Mark why he had absolutely no intention of applying for the new consultancy post.

'As I've told you before, I'd miss my ordinary Obs and Gynae work too much. Oh, I enjoy doing the occasional infertility stuff, but I wouldn't want to do it full time.'

'Not even for extra cash and status?' Mark asked, and Tom shook his head.

'The money might be attractive, but being called 'Mr' instead of 'Dr' isn't the be all and end all for me. Look, if you think it would be such a good job, why don't you apply for it yourself?' he continued. 'You fit in well here, and you've certainly got the qualifications.'

'I've a job lined up in Canada, remember?' Mark pointed out.

'Yes, but that's for a specialist registrar's position, isn't it?' Tom argued back. 'This would be a consultancy.'

Mark looked thoughtful. 'I had the impression Gideon was hoping his brother-in-law might apply?'

'David's certainly not happy at the Merkland, but if you were to tell Gideon you were interested in staying on, I know he'd give your application very serious thought.'

Mark's eyes slid across to Helen's, and she knew what he was thinking. Did she want him to stay? The question was in his eyes as clearly as if he'd actually voiced it, and a month—a week—even ten minutes ago—she would have said go, leave, get out of my life. But now...

Now her mind was a whirl of conflicting emotions, and as Mark continued to gaze at her she could feel heat rising in her cheeks—guilty heat, betraying heat—and he smiled. A slow, understanding smile.

'I don't think staying on at the Belfield would be a good idea,' he said. 'It's a tempting suggestion, but... No, I don't think it would be a good idea. What I want—need—would only work if I moved to a different hospital, another country.'

'We're going to be sorry to see you go, aren't we, Helen?' Tom declared.

'Good grief, is that the time?' she exclaimed. 'I have things—paperwork—to attend to.'

She was gone before Tom could stop her, and he swore under his breath when Mark left soon after, muttering something vague about having a patient to check up on. Dammit, couldn't Helen at least have *pretended* to be sorry that Mark was leaving? The poor bloke would be gone in a fortnight, and it surely wouldn't have killed her to have said something nice to him for a change.

The quicker their new consultant arrived the better, he thought vexedly. With a new consultant on the team he and Helen could take a holiday—a long, leisurely one instead of a snatched weekend grabbed whenever the operating schedule was low. They could go to the cinema, see one of those films the newspapers were always raving about, and maybe then Helen would be less stressed, less difficult to live with.

And she *was* difficult to live with at the moment, he thought with a sigh as he walked out of the staffroom and down the corridor. Everything seemed to annoy her recently. Like those damn flowers. Lord, but it would be a long time before he ever took Gideon's advice about anything again.

'Did your wife like her bouquet, Dr Brooke?'

He turned to see Doris hovering outside her office, and his heart sank. Helen had been right. He'd been a fool to ask Doris to buy them.

'She thought they were lovely,' he lied.

'So they sorted out your little misunderstanding, did they?' Doris continued, her eyes speculative, knowing, and he stiffened.

'I don't know what you mean.'

'Enough said, Doctor.' She smiled, tapping the side of her nose. 'I'm just so pleased that everything's all right. I confess I've been a little bit worried about the two of you, what with Dr Helen's new hairstyle and her more stylish clothes, but she's obviously realised that the grass isn't greener.'

What grass? Tom thought blankly as Doris disappeared back into her office. What the hell was the woman talking about? So Helen had a new haircut, and was apparently wearing more stylish clothes. It didn't mean…

That she was having an affair.

He burst out laughing. It was obviously high time Doris got out more, got a life. OK, so perhaps he and Helen seemed to be doing a lot of arguing but all couples had disagreements. It didn't mean anything.

Then why did she ask you this morning if you loved her? his mind whispered. Why did she get her hair cut, and why—if Doris is to be believed—has she bought herself a whole wardrobe of new clothes?

Because her old clothes are wearing out, he argued back. Because she fancied a new hairstyle for a change. And as for her asking me this morning if I love her…

The laughter on Tom's face died. The night he'd invited Mark round for dinner she'd asked him afterwards if he'd ever been attracted to anybody else. She'd said that as they'd been married for ten years she wouldn't have been surprised if he had. Had she been trying to tell him something?

Desperately he shook his head. No, of course she hadn't been. Helen loved him as much as he loved her, and even if she'd wanted to have an affair she never went anywhere apart from the hospital or the shops.

Which meant it had to be somebody at the hospital.

No, of course it didn't, he told himself savagely. Helen wasn't having an affair. She loved him. She did.

Does she? the insidious little voice persisted. Are you sure about that?

Of course he was sure. He *was*.

And yet as he walked towards the ward he felt a cold chill wrap itself around his heart.

CHAPTER SEVEN

'OH, HELL,' Tom muttered. 'The cancer's not just in Mrs Merrick's cervix—it's spread to her vagina and uterus as well.'

Helen's eyes met his over her theatre mask. 'Is it operable?'

'I can perform a radical hysterectomy, taking out all her pelvic lymph nodes and part of her vagina, but whether that will be enough…' He swore under his breath. 'How did it get to be so advanced? Cervical smears are supposed to detect cancer in its early stages.'

'She hasn't had a smear since her last son was born, and he's seven.'

He shook his head. 'Let me guess. She was always too busy to go for a smear. She had things to do—her sons to look after—and when she started bleeding between her periods she thought it would stop—go away—disappear.'

'Something like that.' Helen nodded.

'Why won't women ever learn?' he exclaimed. 'Bleeding between periods is never something to be ignored, and how long does a cervical smear take? Half an hour tops. One half-hour visit and her GP would have picked up the abnormal cells and we could have killed them before they had a chance to develop.'

'Do you want me to start cancelling some of your less urgent ops?' the theatre sister asked, motioning to one of her staff to start laying out the instruments he was going to need for Mrs Merrick. 'Give you more time with this one?'

'Could you see if you can cadge me some extra operating time first from any of the other departments,

115

Sharon?' he answered. 'I really don't want to cancel anyone's operation if I can help it.'

'Don't forget you've got a clinic this afternoon, Tom,' Helen reminded him. 'And I can't take it for you,' she continued before he could suggest it. 'Gideon's already asked me to do his ward round because he's got a meeting with Admin.'

'This is ridiculous,' he flared. 'We shouldn't need to cancel anybody's operation because of lack of time and operating staff. Well, I'm definitely not cancelling the pelvic repair—the poor woman's leaking urine like a sieve. And I'm certainly not cancelling the ovarian cyst.'

'What about Mrs Foster?'

He said something unprintable about Mrs Foster, then shook his head. 'I'll have to squeeze her in somehow. Heaven knows what damage she's possibly done with her wallpapering activities. OK, we'll do Mrs Merrick, the pelvic repair, the ovarian cyst and Mrs Foster. Sharon, if you wangle me some extra operating time we'll do the D and C, the sterilisation and the prolapse. If not, they'll have to be cancelled.'

'You're never going to be finished for your two o'clock clinic even with those cancellations,' Helen pointed out.

'If my clinic starts late, then it starts late,' he said tightly. 'Sharon, get on the phone and see what you can do for me.'

The theatre sister hurried away and Barry, the anaesthetist, looked up from his monitors. 'Mrs Merrick's well under, Tom. Ready to roll whenever you are.'

'I'll be a hell of a lot readier when we get our new consultant,' Tom said as he reached for a scalpel.

He expected Helen to say 'Amen' but she didn't. In fact, she'd been remarkably offhand about the addition of a new member of staff since Gideon had given them the good news on Tuesday. Oh, she'd said it was marvellous, tremendous, would make such a difference, but he had the oddest impression that she was just saying the words, that her thoughts were elsewhere.

Probably working up the courage to tell you she doesn't love you any more, his mind whispered as he made an incision into Yvonne's abdomen.

No!

The word seared through his brain so loudly that for a second he wondered if he'd actually said it out loud, but nobody in the operating theatre looked up, nobody gazed questioningly at him.

Damn Doris and her insidious innuendo, he thought savagely as he parted the skin round the incision he'd made. These thoughts—fears—would never have occurred to him—not for a second—if she hadn't placed the seed of doubt in his mind, and now it was there, working its poison, twisting everything Helen had said and done recently.

'BP 120 over 80, temp normal, heart rate normal,' Barry announced, adjusting the dials on his monitors.

Tom nodded. 'Clamps, please.'

Helen handed them to him, and he shot her a glance. If Doris was right, surely he would have noticed—seen the tell-tale signs?

He wasn't naïve. He knew that some of the staff at the Belfield were involved in affairs. Affairs that almost always began because as medics they all saw so much pain and heartache in their work, and it was often easier to talk to a colleague than to anybody else. But the only men Helen saw regularly were himself, Gideon and Barry. She saw Mark, too, of course, but considering she was barely civil to him he could discount him immediately.

'Drain,' he demanded.

Helen eased the suction into place and a frown pleated his forehead as he watched her. Haematology. She went down to Haematology a lot, and yet when Mark had asked if she could hurry up his blood tests on Mrs Dukakis, she'd been strangely reluctant to go. Was that because she felt an attraction towards the head of the department?

Oh, get a grip, Tom, he told himself. The head of Haematology's sixty if he's a day, with a paunch you could rest your coffee-cup on.

'Sorry, Doctor, but no luck with the extra operating time,' Sharon said as she rejoined them. 'In fact, I wouldn't care to repeat what some of the departments said when I asked.'

Helen chuckled, a deep throaty sound that tore at Tom's heart.

Perhaps he should just ask her outright. Say 'Look, are you having an affair?' But did he really want to know if she was? Did he really want her to tell him she didn't love him any more? She was his whole world—had been since the day he'd met her—and without her…

'Sorry, Sharon,' he muttered as the instrument she was holding out to him slipped through his fingers and clattered to the floor.

'No problem, Doctor,' she replied, selecting another one.

Helen clearly thought there was. Helen looked puzzled, and he knew why. In all the years he'd been a surgeon he'd never dropped an instrument. Never.

Concentrate, Tom, he told himself, concentrate. OK, so you've hardly slept for the last two nights with Doris's words running round and round in your head, but an operating theatre's no place for private worries. There's too much at stake, and in Mrs Merrick's case it's her whole future.

'What are her chances?' Helen asked after he'd performed Yvonne's radical hysterectomy, removing her pelvic lymph nodes and as much of her vagina as he hoped was necessary.

'I don't know,' he said wearily as he followed her into the changing rooms to grab a quick shower and a set of fresh theatre scrubs before their next patient was wheeled in. 'She has four children, you said?'

'The oldest is fourteen, the youngest seven.'

He stabbed his fingers through his hair. 'Radiotherapy will help but… Realistically I'd have to put the chances of her still being alive in five years at fifty-fifty.'

'I've heard worse odds,' she said gently, and he grimaced.

'It's so unnecessary, Helen, so damned unnecessary. If only she'd gone to her GP sooner—the minute she noticed the bleeding. If only she hadn't kept putting it off.'

'Saddest words in the world, aren't they?' Helen murmured, pulling her theatre top over her head. '"If only."'

I don't love you any more are even sadder, he thought, his eyes drawn to the high curve of her breasts encased in a white lace bra, the darkened tips of her nipples just showing through the fabric. She was so beautiful—so very beautiful. When had he last told her that?

He couldn't remember, and maybe that was the trouble. Maybe he'd assumed too much, taken too much for granted over the years.

'Helen—'

'We'd better hurry up and shower,' she interrupted. 'Your pelvic repair job's down, and if you want to do the ovarian cyst and Mrs Foster as well…'

She disappeared into the shower cubicle without waiting for his reply, and unhappily Tom stared after her. When they'd first got married they'd actually shared a theatre shower once. It had been against every hospital rule but, then, so had a lot of the things they'd done in sluice rooms and store cupboards. They hadn't cared. They'd been so much in love, so happy. How had it all gone wrong?

It hasn't, his heart insisted. *She still loves you as much as you love her. You're just overreacting, panicking unnecessarily.*

But he wasn't. Deep down inside him he knew that he

wasn't. He was losing her. Slowly but surely he was losing her.

He got through the pelvic floor repair operation and the ovarian cyst on autopilot. Somehow he managed to ask for the right instruments, didn't drop anything, didn't make any mistakes, but it was a relief when his last patient was wheeled in.

'Do I recognise this face, or ought I to start getting out more?' Barry said as he adjusted the oxygen dials.

'It's Mrs Foster,' Helen replied. 'She was in a month ago for a hysterectomy.'

'Likes hospitals, does she?' The anaesthetist grinned. 'Or is it my magnetic personality?'

'Don't I wish,' Helen said ruefully. 'I'm afraid Mrs Foster is a DIY enthusiast. She came in with severe stomach pains two days ago after she'd finished wallpapering her sitting room.'

Barry's eyebrows shot up to his mask. 'I wouldn't call her a DIY enthusiast. I'd call her an idiot.'

'You and me both.' Helen chuckled. 'What's the damage, Tom?'

'Not as bad as I thought, though it would have been better if she hadn't done it at all,' he replied. 'She's torn some of her vaginal stitches. How's things your end, Barry?'

'No problems. She's sleeping like a baby.'

'That must be a first,' Helen said with feeling, and the anaesthetist laughed.

'One of nature's complainers, is she?'

'Founding member of the group, I'd say,' Helen replied, and Tom glanced suspiciously from her to Barry.

Not Barry. It couldn't be Barry. OK, so he was single, mid to late thirties, but wasn't he dating one of the theatre nurses? Helen had probably told him which one, but for the life of him he couldn't remember. He wished now that he could.

'Swab,' he said more sharply than he'd intended, and saw the puzzled look appear in Helen's eyes again.

Strange how he'd forgotten how brown her eyes were. Like liquid amber. It had been one of the first things he'd noticed about her. That, and her ready smile. Her smile hadn't been much in evidence lately, he thought sadly, and he should have noticed. Should have realised why.

'BP's up,' Barry declared. 'One-twenty over 85. No, make that 130 over 90.'

'She's very clammy,' Sharon observed. 'Neck veins slightly swollen.'

'Pulse erratic.' That was Helen, her eyes suddenly concerned above her mask.

'Temps going up, too,' Barry chipped in, 'and her heart rate—'

The high-pitched monotone of the heart monitor cut off the rest of what he'd been about to say, and the calm of the operating theatre was shattered in an instant.

'My God, myocardial infarction,' Sharon gasped. 'She's arrested, Tom!'

Quickly Tom hit Mrs Foster squarely in the centre of her chest with his fist. Sometimes that simple action was enough to restart a heart that had stopped after a heart attack, but in this case Helen shook her head.

'No tracing—no activity—nothing,' she declared, her eyes fixed on the heart monitor.

'OK, paddles, conducting gel, 200 joules,' Tom ordered. With the efficiency of a well-oiled machine everyone sprang to their allotted places and Tom placed the paddles on either side of Mrs Foster's chest. 'So you think you can die on me, do you, Mrs Foster?' he murmured. 'Swan up to the pearly gates to plague St Peter instead of me? Well, think again. Everybody back.'

As one they all stepped back from the operating table, the electrical switch was thrown and Mrs Foster's body arched convulsively, then slumped heavily back down.

'No change,' Helen reported, her voice tense.

'Being difficult as usual, are we, Mrs Foster?' Tom said grimly. 'Well, I'm the surgeon and I call the shots here, and you are not going to die on me. Three hundred joules, Sharon.'

'Three hundred joules,' she repeated. 'OK, everybody clear.'

Again Tom placed the paddles on either side of Mrs Foster's chest, and again her body convulsed.

'Slight tracing visible,' Helen declared. 'Too erratic— No, it's starting to even out—becoming more regular— you've got her, Tom.'

A collective sigh of relief went up, and Tom glanced across at Helen.

'Five will get you ten that the first thing she complains about when she wakes up is the bruising on her chest.'

She laughed a little shakily. 'Hey, you should know by now that I never bet on certainties.'

And I shouldn't have let my mind wander, he thought as he rapidly repaired the stitches Mrs Foster had burst when she'd been wallpapering. If I hadn't been thinking about Helen—

No. Nobody could have been prepared for Mrs Foster having a heart attack. It happened. It happened in young, fit people as well as middle-aged, plump women with an attitude problem.

'Are you OK?' Helen asked when Mrs Foster was finally wheeled through to Recovery.

'I've had better mornings,' he admitted.

'She'll be all right,' she said encouragingly. 'She's too damned cussed to die.'

A smile creased one corner of his mouth, then was gone. Barry would stay with Mrs Foster, monitoring her until he was sure she was emerging from the anaesthesia as she should, and with luck she should suffer no after-effects. She'd have to be told about what had happened, of course, be warned about her diet and lifestyle, but, knowing Mrs Foster, she wouldn't pay a blind bit of notice.

He just wished that there was some medical procedure he could perform which would turn the clock back for him. Back to the days when he and Helen had been happy. Back to when he'd been secure and certain of her love.

'Have you time for lunch?' he asked after they'd showered and changed.

She shook her head. 'Neither of us do. You've got a clinic, and I've got Gideon's ward round to do, remember?'

Why did they never seem to have any time any more? When they'd been students there'd always been time. Time for laughing, time for loving, time for making plans.

And what plans they'd had. They were both going to be consultants by the time they were thirty-five. They would have two beautiful children, a nice house, a top-of-the-range car. They'd achieved so little of their dreams. Oh, they had the children, but the house they lived in was rented and their car was second-hand. It hadn't seemed to matter before when they'd been secure in one another's love, but now…

'I'm going to try to get away early tonight, Helen,' he said as they walked through the swing doors that led into Obs and Gynae. 'Be home at a reasonable time.'

'Famous last words,' she said. 'The minute either of us says that, an emergency always comes in just as we're about to leave.'

She was right, it usually did, but he couldn't let her walk away knowing that by the time he got home she'd probably be fast asleep in bed.

'I really like your new hairstyle, Helen,' he said quickly. 'It's lovely.'

She looked startled. Startled and wary. Did that mean he rarely paid her compliments? It probably did.

'That's a new skirt, too, isn't it?' he ploughed on. 'And a new blouse?'

'Tom, you bought me this blouse last Christmas, and I've had the skirt for two years.'

Oh, great. Zero out of ten for observation, Tom. Minus zero, in fact.

'Well, you look very nice,' he said, only to groan inwardly. Jerk. Idiot. 'Nice' is a taboo word, remember? The verbal equivalent of waving a red rag in front of her face. 'I mean, you look lovely, very lovely.' Oh, even better, Tom, he thought, seeing her shoulders stiffen. Three 'lovelies'. That's another zero out of ten—this time for originality. 'Helen—'

'Why are you paying me compliments, Tom?'

'Does there have to be a reason?' he protested. 'You're my wife, and if I want to say nice—' damn, he'd used that word again '—things about you, why shouldn't I?'

'No reason, I suppose,' she muttered.

Lord, but she looked tense. Tense, and edgy, and inexplicably defensive. What had he done wrong now? All he'd tried to do was pay her a few compliments and yet from the way she was looking at him you'd have thought he'd suddenly grown two heads.

'Helen, listen—'

'Are you going to be much longer, Dr Brooke?' Doris asked, appearing at her office door. 'Only you're already more than an hour late for your clinic and your patients are beginning to get a bit restless.'

'And as I'm busy right now they'll just have to damn well stay restless,' he retorted.

'I see. Right, Dr Brooke,' she replied, disappearing back into her office but not before she'd glanced from him to Helen with a knowing look that set his teeth on edge.

'Helen—'

'Brilliant, Tom, really brilliant, Tom,' she declared tartly. 'Not content with telling Doris on Monday that we've had one row, you've now gone and shown her we're having another one.'

Were they rowing? He hadn't realised they were, but then he didn't seem to know anything any more.

'Helen, if I've messed up again, I'm sorry, but…' He thrust his fingers through his brown hair with frustration. How could he say, 'Look, are you having an affair—are you attracted to somebody else?' If she wasn't she'd think he was an idiot, but if she was… 'Are you on call tonight?'

'Of course I am,' she exclaimed. 'I'm on call every night this week.'

'Unless Mark plays the good Samaritan for you again,' he said, hoping for a smile, but she didn't smile back. Say it, his mind insisted. For God's sake, just say it—ask her—find out. 'Helen…Helen, we need to talk.'

'You mean about a patient?'

'No, I don't mean about a bloody patient,' he snapped, then bit his lip as she flinched. She wasn't meeting his gaze. Why wasn't she meeting his gaze? 'Helen we never talk any more.'

'Of course we do.'

'No, we don't, not about us. We talk about the children, our work, our patients, but we don't talk about *us*.'

She looked at the floor, at his white coat, at everything but him. 'I don't understand what you mean.'

'You must do,' he insisted. 'Helen, our marriage—'

'I don't have time for this right now, Tom,' she interrupted. 'I've a ward round to do, and you've got a clinic.'

She was backing away from him and she looked unhappy, and edgy, and… Guilty. Did she look guilty, or was it just his imagination—Doris's poisonous words—making him think that she did?

'Helen—'

'Later, Tom. Not now—later.'

He couldn't make her stay and talk to him. He couldn't force her into the store cupboard, and keep her there until she told him what he wanted—needed—to know. He had patients waiting. Patients who needed him. And no matter how much he wanted to go after Helen, to beg her to tell him what was wrong, right now those patients came first.

So he buried himself in his work, listened to the worries and fears of the women who had been referred to him. But the minute his clinic was over he was heading for the door.

'What about the files, Doctor?' Doris called after him. 'Do you want me to file the notes of the patients you've seen this afternoon or can I leave them until tomorrow?'

For a second he was tempted to tell her exactly what she could do with his notes but common sense and tact prevailed.

'I'll file them for you—you get off home.'

'Are you sure?' she said, already reaching for her bag and coat. 'After all, it's my job, not yours, and even though I'm supposed to go off duty at half past five, and it's already half past six…'

'I'll do it, Doris,' he said firmly.

And he would, but not right now. The minute Doris had gone he was going to the ward. Helen would be getting ready to leave, and if he was lucky he might be able to have a brief word with her, apologise for whatever he'd done wrong.

That, at least, was his plan, but though Helen was the first person he saw when he entered the ward, Gideon collared him before he could get anywhere near her.

'Helen told me about Mrs Foster,' the consultant declared. 'Talk about drama!'

'It was certainly a shock,' Tom replied, trying to edge away only to see the consultant come after him. 'But I understand she's stable now.'

'I took a look through her records when Helen told me what had happened,' Gideon continued, 'and there's nothing to suggest she might be an at-risk patient.'

'I think it was just one of those things,' Tom said, desperately trying to catch Helen's eye, but Mark was talking to her, explaining something judging by the way she was listening to him.

'Probably.' The consultant nodded. 'Actually, she reminds me a lot of a patient I had years ago—Elspeth Mackay. Elspeth had a hysterectomy, too, and you'll never believe what she did when she was discharged. You see, Mrs Mackay's husband was a farmer, and…'

What on earth was Mark saying to Helen? Tom wondered as Gideon recounted his tale of Mrs Mackay. Whatever it was, she didn't seem to like it. She looked uncomfortable, and ill at ease, and then he saw the reason why. Mark was holding her hand. Holding it and murmuring something in her ear. Big mistake, mate, he thought wryly. Any second now Helen is going to give you one hell of an earful. But she didn't.

Instead, she looked up at Mark and shook her head. Mark said something else, and as Tom watched a slow blush of colour creep across Helen's cheeks the bottom fell out of his world.

Not Mark. Not his one-time best friend. Dammit, Helen didn't even *like* him. She was always telling him he was a flirt and a womaniser, and yet—why was she letting him hold her hand? Why was she blushing and gazing up at him like a teenager on her first date?

'And when Elspeth told me she'd been helping her husband with the lambing…' Gideon laughed '…well, it all became crystal clear.'

Too clear, Tom thought. He should have seen it before, should have guessed it might happen. Back in med school Mark had always been poaching his girlfriends for a joke, but it wasn't a joke now, and Helen wasn't his girlfriend, she was his wife.

'Gideon, I need a favour,' he said quickly. 'A big one. I'm scheduled to work tonight until eight. Could you stand in for me—let me off early?'

The consultant looked surprised, and not at all happy. 'It's a bit short notice.'

'I wouldn't ask if it wasn't important,' Tom insisted, noticing that Helen was walking towards the ward door and Mark was staring after her with an expression on his handsome face which made him long to rearrange those, oh, so perfect features.

'I'd like to help you out, Tom, I really would,' Gideon said, 'but Annie and I are going to the cinema tonight.'

'We'll go another evening,' the junior doctor interrupted, appearing at their side without warning.

'But you said you were really looking forward to tonight,' Gideon protested. 'You said—'

'Forget what I said,' Annie declared. 'Let Tom leave early, Gideon.'

The consultant looked bemused. Annie didn't. How much did she know? Enough, it seemed, judging by the pointed look she was giving her husband.

'Well, if Annie says it's all right,' Gideon began, and Tom didn't wait to hear any more. He was out the ward and running. Running to catch up with Helen. Running as though his whole life depended on it, and right now he thought it did.

'And he gave you the rest of the evening off—just like that?' Helen said for the third time that evening as she slid the lamb chops off the grill, took the baked potatoes out of the microwave and put the bowl of salad in the centre of the kitchen table.

'He said something about me looking tired.'

'John, take some salad as well as potatoes,' Helen ordered. 'It's good for you.'

'It's rabbit food—'

'It's still good for you. Emma, how many times have I told you? No comics at the table.'

'It's not a comic, Mum, it's a geographical magazine.

There's some really great pictures in it about Australia and some of them are of places Mark told us about. When's he going to come back again for a meal? I think he's great.'

'Emma, will you sit on that seat properly instead of bouncing around like you've got ants in your pants?' Helen ordered. 'I've no idea when Mark might come back. He's a very busy man.'

Not that busy, Tom thought sourly. Not too busy to seduce my wife.

How far had it gone? Not that far, he guessed, hoped. Helen was too straight, too honest to be able to keep something like that from him. If she was sleeping with Mark, surely he would know?

They had to talk, but never had a meal seemed so interminable. Never had Tom so longed for his children to go to bed, but even after they'd watched their allotted amount of television they showed no sign of moving. Emma was too full of excitement because she'd been chosen to be a member of the girls' swimming team at school, and John was equally determined to extract more pocket money out of him to buy some new computer game that 'everybody' had.

'OK, time for bed,' Helen eventually declared, to his relief.

They didn't go right away—they never did—but at long last, after the usual obligatory moans and groans, Emma and John finally made their way upstairs.

'Peace at last,' he said, switching off the television.

'Do you want a coffee, or tea, or anything?' Helen asked, and when he shook his head she sat down beside him on the sofa, reached for a magazine and began flicking through it,

Now, he thought. Now's the time, now's the moment, but what could he say? He'd never possessed Mark's charm, his good looks, his way with words. How could he convince Helen that he loved her when he was never going to be able to make the kind of flattering speeches that tripped so easily off Mark's tongue?

Show her, his heart suggested. Show her you care, that the love is still there.

'Helen…' He cleared his throat, and started again. 'Will you come to bed with me?'

Was it his imagination or had her grip on the magazine tightened?

'I'm on call tonight, remember?' she replied.

He almost said 'We might get lucky' until he remembered what had happened the last time he'd said that. How the whole evening had gone right down the tube.

'Helen, please.' Dear Lord, he was begging. Begging his own wife to make love to him. Well, he had no pride, not where she was concerned. 'Helen, it's been so long since we made love, and…and I need you.' Slowly she lowered the magazine, and to his utter horror he could see tears sparkling in her eyes. Oh, hell, could he never get it right? 'Helen, I'm sorry. Oh, love, don't—please, don't cry.'

Desperately he reached for her, and she met him halfway, clinging to him with an almost frantic desperation.

'Kiss me, Tom,' she muttered into his chest. 'Don't talk—don't say anything. Just…kiss me.'

With a ragged groan he took her mouth, teasing her lips gently at first, but she didn't seem to want him to be gentle. Her whole body might be trembling beneath his fingers, but her lips were firm, demanding, almost as though she was seeking an answer to something, and he returned the pressure of her lips with equal intensity, plundering her mouth, locking his fingers in her hair to bring her even closer.

'Helen—'

'No words—no words,' she gasped, sliding herself onto his lap, straddling him with her thighs, pressing herself hard against him so he could feel her heat. 'Make love to me, Tom. Just make love to me.'

She dug her fingers deep into his shoulders as he unbuttoned her blouse, then slipped her bra from her. Arched against him, whimpering, when he took first one hardened peak into his mouth and suckled it, then the other, and convulsed jerkily when his fingers slid up under her skirt to touch and caress her warm dampness.

Damn Mark for all eternity, he thought savagely as he lowered her onto the sofa and reached for the zip of his trousers. She was *his* wife, not Mark's. *His* love, not Mark's. But as he drew her closer a groan of frustration was torn from him as the phone suddenly rang.

'Ignore it,' he begged, his voice raw with need. 'Pretend we didn't hear it.'

'I can't—you know I can't,' she gasped, rolling out from under him, already reaching for her bra.

It was the hospital, of course. He knew with a certain grim inevitability even before she lifted the phone that it was going to be the hospital.

'I'll wait up for you,' he said as she lifted the car keys, but she shook her head. 'There's no point. I could be hours.'

She was right, but that didn't stop his body protesting, demanding release, as he heard her drive away.

Why couldn't the switchboard have waited an hour—half an hour—even ten minutes—before they'd rung? If it could only have waited, Helen and he would have made love and then he was sure everything would have been all right again.

But, no, it had to ring, and Helen had gone.

Slowly he went upstairs and into their bedroom where the empty bed seemed to mock him. Perhaps if Helen got back early from the hospital…

His lips twisted. The way his luck was running at the moment he'd be lucky if he saw her by breakfast-time, and with a sigh he opened the wardrobe to hang up his jacket, only to frown as his eyes caught sight of a gold carrier bag stuffed at the very back of the wardrobe.

Curiously he hauled it out, but as he stared down at the bag his frown gave way to a smile. Helen must have bought herself something very expensive and was trying to pluck up the courage to tell him. Should he find out what it was, or let her surprise him? His conscience told him to let her surprise him, but common sense told him that if he at least knew what it was he wouldn't look so much of an idiot by complimenting her on something she'd had for years.

Quickly he reached into the bag but as he drew out the contents a hard lump formed in his throat.

It was a nightdress. A scarlet nightdress so sheer and fine it was practically transparent. A scarlet nightdress so blatantly sexy that any red-blooded male who saw Helen in it would have been turned on instantly.

But she hadn't bought it for him.

As he crushed the flimsy material between his fingers, he knew without a shadow of a doubt that she had bought it to wear for Mark.

CHAPTER EIGHT

'WELL, all I can say is there's got to be something far wrong with a hospital if a person can come into it with a stomach ache and end up having a heart attack,' Mrs Foster exclaimed, her plump cheeks quivering with indignation. 'Now, I'm not one to complain, Doctor…'

Yeah, right, Helen thought, schooling her features into an expression of solicitude with difficulty. Mrs Foster had done nothing *but* complain from the day she'd met her, and since she'd recovered from her heart attack in the theatre last Thursday she'd been impossible.

'And as for Dr Brooke's suggestion that I should lose some weight,' Mrs Foster continued imperiously. 'What does my weight have to do with anything?'

'Quite a lot, actually,' Helen replied. 'You see, people who are overweight are often more prone to heart attacks. The excess weight puts a strain on their heart, and—'

'My mother never weighed any less than fourteen stone and she was ninety-five when she died. All this talk of diet and exercise… If you want my opinion, it's just an excuse to cover up sloppy surgery. If my hysterectomy had been carried out properly in the first place…'

Helen groaned inwardly as Mrs Foster launched into her by now all-too-familiar diatribe against the Belfield in general, and Tom in particular. Sometimes Helen wondered why she bothered—why any of them bothered.

Because of people like Yvonne Merrick, she thought, noticing the woman smiling sympathetically at her from down the ward. OK, so the woman had been foolish to ignore her symptoms for so long but she couldn't help but feel that Yvonne deserved her attention a hell of a lot more than Mrs Foster did. If Mrs Foster followed their recommendations, there was no reason why she shouldn't live to the same age as her mother, but Yvonne's future was uncertain in the extreme.

'Could I have a word with you, please, Doctor?'

Helen glanced round to see Gideon standing behind her, and tried hard not to look too relieved. 'I'm afraid you'll have to excuse me, Mrs Foster—'

'And that's another thing that's wrong with this hospital,' the woman called after her as she walked away. 'The staffing levels in it are atrocious. There's never enough nurses and doctors to attend to our needs. You're always rushing off somewhere.'

'Mostly to get as far away from her as possible,' Gideon commented the moment they were out of earshot, and Helen sighed.

'I know we're not supposed to let our personal feelings get in the way of our work, but…'

'Mrs Foster gets right up your nose?' Gideon smiled ruefully. 'As far as I'm concerned, the sooner she's discharged, the better.'

'When will she be able to go home?'

'Another week—twelve days probably—always supposing one of us doesn't murder her first.'

Helen chuckled. 'Did you really want to talk to me or were you just performing a rescue mission?'

Gideon looked slightly uncomfortable. 'Actually, I did want a word. It's Tom, Helen. He looks quite dreadful.'

He did, and any gratitude Helen might have felt towards the consultant for rescuing her evaporated in an instant.

'I'm not surprised he looks dreadful considering all the extra shifts you've been dumping on him,' she said tartly. 'It's not on, Gideon, it really isn't. He's practically living at the Belfield—'

'Hey, it's not my fault,' Gideon protested. 'I haven't been forcing him to work extra shifts. He volunteered.'

'Tom *volunteered?*' she repeated. 'But—'

'I thought…' Gideon flushed slightly. 'I thought perhaps the two of you were in some sort of financial trouble, perhaps needed the extra cash.'

'No, we're not in any financial trouble,' she said, bewildered. At least, nothing Tom had told her about. 'Gideon—'

'I told him this morning that enough was enough. In fact, I've insisted he does no more evening or night work for a month, and nearly got my head in my hands for my trouble. What's wrong with him, Helen?'

She wished she knew. Last week, when he'd reached for her—suggested they make love—she'd thought all her stupid fears and doubts about their marriage had been just that—stupid. OK, so she'd known that the mere act of making love wasn't going to provide the answer to all their problems, but the fact that he'd desired her had at least proved the attraction between them was still there. But since then he'd been so distant, snapping at the children, barely exchanging a word with her.

She'd thought it was simply because he was exhausted by all the extra shifts Gideon had given him, and to hear now that he'd actually volunteered for them…

'Are you sure about him volunteering?' she said uncertainly. 'You couldn't possibly have misunderstood?'

'It's a bit difficult to misunderstand a request for extra shifts, Helen.'

He was right, it was, but why would Tom volunteer? It made no sense unless…

Unless he's trying to avoid you, her heart whispered, but why would he want to make love to her one night, then deliberately distance himself from her from then on?

Guilt, her heart answered. He felt guilty that night about not loving you any more and decided to make love to you one more time before telling you that he was leaving you.

It made sense. It made horrible, awful sense.

'Oh, heck, Helen, I'm sorry,' Gideon said quickly, consternation on his face as a small sob came from her. 'I shouldn't have said anything—me and my big mouth. Forget I said anything. Forget I even mentioned the subject.'

He took off before she could stop him, disappearing out of the ward like a panic-stricken rabbit, and a wobbly smile touched her lips as she watched him go. Poor Gideon. Never had she seen him look quite so embarrassed, and all because of one small sob. She wondered what he would have done if she'd burst into tears. Gone into orbit, probably.

Tom was exactly the same. He hated seeing her cry, too. Or at least he used to, she thought as she walked slowly down the ward. Now she wasn't sure how he would react to anything she did any more. Now she didn't even know if he loved her any more.

'Thanks, Doctor,' Yvonne said as Helen bent to retrieve the book which had slipped off her bed.

'Alternative Treatments for Cervical Cancer,' Helen observed, squinting at the title before she handed it back. 'Don't you think it's a bit early to be thinking of that? You haven't even had your radiotherapy yet.'

'My husband brought it in for me.' Yvonne grimaced slightly. 'He's panicking a bit, you see.'

Yvonne didn't appear to be. In fact, if anything, Yvonne had been far too bright and cheerful since Tom had told her how far the cancer had spread. Helen guessed she was keeping a tight lid on her emotions, but it wasn't healthy. The more Yvonne bottled things up, the more catastrophic it was going to be when she finally let go.

'And you,' Helen asked, perching on the end of Yvonne's bed. 'How are you?'

'Oh, I'm fine,' the woman replied with a smile that didn't reach her eyes. 'I mean, the success rate for treating people with cancer has improved dramatically recently, hasn't it?'

'It has indeed.' Helen nodded. 'In fact—'

'And just because my cancer has spread so far, and you've had to take away so much of my insides, doesn't mean that I... It doesn't mean I'm necessarily going to...to...'

'Die?' Helen suggested gently, and saw the woman swallow convulsively. 'Yvonne, listen to me—'

'I'm just being stupid, aren't I?' Yvonne interrupted, her voice thick. 'Feeling sorry for myself like this... It's not going to get me anywhere, is it? I...I've got to be positive—look to the future—but sometimes...sometimes...'

'Let it out, Yvonne,' Helen urged as the woman bit her lip. 'Stop being so brave and noble, and just let it out.'

She did. Tears suddenly began trickling down Yvonne's cheeks. Tears that became racking sobs. Helen held her tightly, murmuring words she guessed Yvonne scarcely heard but hoped she took some comfort from.

'I'm so sorry,' Yvonne gulped when her tears were spent. 'You must think I'm such a fool...'

'Yvonne, everyone's frightened when they're told they have cancer,' Helen said softly. 'It's not a sign of weakness to cry.'

'I just wish I'd gone to my GP sooner. If I hadn't kept on putting it off, and putting it off...'

'I'm afraid no amount of wishing and hoping can change what's happened,' Helen murmured. 'All you can do is to look forward and not back, and the surgery Dr Brooke performed has at least given you a fighting chance.'

'That's what your husband said. He's such a nice man— isn't he?' Yvonne said tremulously. 'Oh, I know most of the women in the ward think Dr Lorimer's the best thing since sliced bread, but I prefer your husband. He's honest, and solid, and you know where you are with him.'

I don't, Helen thought as she settled Mrs Merrick down. All I know is that I'm miserable and unhappy, and I don't know what to do about it.

Then confront him, her mind whispered. OK, so maybe you won't like what he says, but surely anything's better than this uncertainty, this doubt?

'Liz, do you have any idea where Tom is?' she asked, seeing the sister hurry past her with a bedpan.

'Last time I saw him he was heading for the staffroom,' Liz threw over her shoulder.

Helen glanced down at her watch. His morning clinic must have finished early. He'd be grabbing a quick coffee before he joined Gideon in Theatre, and although the staffroom was hardly the ideal place for a private conversation it would have to do.

Tom clearly didn't agree with her. His face stiffened into tight, grim lines when she appeared, but she'd come this far and she wasn't going to back down now.

'Tom, I have to talk to you.'

He was already getting to his feet. 'I'm afraid I don't have the time—'

'Then make the time,' she insisted. 'Tom, you said yourself that we don't talk any more. That all we ever talk about is the hospital, our patients, the children. And you were right.'

For a second she thought he was going to sit down again, but he didn't. 'Can't we talk about this later?'

'*When?*' she demanded. 'You only come home nowadays to sleep—'

'It's not my fault I'm so busy.'

The blatancy of his lie took her breath away, but she wasn't going to lose her temper. She refused to allow herself to lose her temper.

'Oh, really?' she said as calmly as she could. 'Well, that's very interesting when Gideon's just told me you've been volunteering to work extra shifts.'

A guilty tide of colour rushed over his cheeks.

'Gideon had no right to talk about me behind my back,' he flared, and she shook her head.

'Tom, he has every right. He's worried about you. *I'm* worried about you.'

'Are you—are you really?' he said, and her jaw dropped.

'Of course I am. Tom, you're my husband—'

'I'm glad you can still remember that.'

'Remember it?' she echoed, bewildered. 'What the hell's that supposed to mean?'

His eyes met hers for a second with a look she didn't understand, then he muttered, 'Nothing.'

'Don't you ''Nothing'' me, Tom Brooke,' she exclaimed. 'It's not nothing that you seem hell-bent on working yourself into the ground. It's not nothing that you seem to prefer to be at the Belfield instead of home with me and the kids.'

'Maybe if I thought you actually wanted me there I might come home more often.'

'*Wanted* you there?' she gasped. Then all the anger and confusion she'd been trying to keep in check exploded. 'OK, that does it. I don't know what you're talking about, but—'

'Neither do I, but if the two of you don't lower your voices I reckon the entire hospital is soon going to find out.'

Helen bit her lip savagely as she turned to see Mark standing in the doorway. Right now she didn't give a damn if the whole world knew that she and Tom were in the middle of a blazing row. All she knew was that Mark had lousy timing, really lousy timing.

Tom clearly thought so, too. In fact, if the look he threw his friend had been any more searing Mark would have been toast.

'Is there something we can do for you, Mark, or are you

just here to make smart remarks?' he said, his lips a thin white line of anger.

'I wanted a coffee if it's all the same to you, and to ask Helen something,' he replied.

He didn't just have lousy timing, Helen thought as she watched in amazement as Mark made himself a coffee, then sipped it with obvious relish. He was also completely impervious to atmosphere. How could he stand there casually drinking his coffee when you could have cut the air in the room with a knife? If she'd been in his shoes she'd have been out of the staffroom, fast.

'What did you want to talk to me about, Mark?' she said, hoping he might take the hint, finish his coffee and go.

'I was wondering if you'd like to come out to dinner with me tonight.'

'I'm afraid we couldn't possibly get a babysitter at such short notice,' she said dismissively. 'The agency I normally use is booked up weeks in advance—'

'I wasn't asking Tom out to dinner, Helen. Just you.'

Was he out of his mind? Her eyes flashed across to Tom in consternation. What the hell was he doing, asking her out in front of her husband?

'Mark—'

'You see, I'm leaving the Belfield on Sunday,' he continued smoothly, 'and it occurred to me that I really must do something to thank you for that marvellous meal you cooked for me. Tom and I are old friends so there's no need for me to thank him, but I'd very much like to show you my appreciation.'

Lord, but his nerve was breathtaking, she thought as he gazed at her, all wide-eyed innocence. His invitation had absolutely nothing to do with the meal she'd cooked for him. He knew it, and she knew it, too.

'It's very kind of you, Mark,' she began, hoping her

cheeks weren't as red as they felt, 'but there's really no need.'

'I insist,' he declared. 'It seems the least I can do in the circumstances.'

Why wasn't Tom saying something? Why didn't he simply tell Mark his invitation was unnecessary? Surely he must know that she didn't want to—couldn't—go out with Mark, but he was just standing there, gazing at them both, his face devoid of all emotion.

'Like I said, it's a kind thought, Mark,' she repeated, 'but you don't need to thank me by taking me out to dinner, and I'm sure Tom would agree, don't you, Tom?'

Her husband's grey eyes met hers, blank and expressionless. 'It's up to you, Helen.'

Up to her? Didn't he care if she went out with his friend? Was he so blind, or so stupid or so uncaring, that it didn't occur to him that it might be wrong for her to go out with such a devastatingly handsome man?

'Tom—'

'Your choice, Helen—your decision,' he said, and as she stared back at him a wave of hurt anger flooded through her.

He didn't care. He didn't care what she did, where she went or with who. Well, all right, then. If that was how he felt she'd damn well go out with Mark and to hell with him.

'Tonight, you said, Mark?' she said tightly.

'I understand Tom has the evening off so there'd be no need for you to get a babysitter,' he observed.

Her eyes met her husband's once more, hoping for a flare of anger, a spark of interest, but there was nothing, and her jaw set.

'Tonight would be lovely, Mark.'

He smiled. 'I thought it might be. Liz tells me Stephano's is the best restaurant in town, but if you'd like to go somewhere else…?'

Stephano's was indeed the best restaurant in Glasgow. It was also the place men took women they wanted to impress. Well, if she was going out with Mark she had no intention of going to some hole-in-the-wall café.

'Stephano's sounds wonderful,' she replied, forcing a smile to her lips.

'Terrific.' Mark nodded. 'I'll pick you up at eight, shall I?'

'Eight will be fine,' she said, daring her husband to object—longing for him to object—but Tom didn't say a word.

He was thinking plenty, though, as he watched Helen leave the staffroom. Thinking plenty, and praying he'd be able to keep the lid on his temper long enough for him to say what he wanted to say.

It wasn't easy. In fact, he only managed to keep silent until the staffroom was safely closed, then he rounded on Mark, his face dark with fury. 'I want to say only one thing to you—keep your hands off my wife.'

Mark's eyebrows rose. 'I beg your pardon?'

'So you should, but morality's never been one of your strong points, has it?'

'Hey, Tom, my old friend—'

'Don't play the innocent with me, Mark,' Tom said, his tone dangerous. 'It didn't suit you ten years ago and it sure as hell doesn't suit you now. Helen is my wife—'

'Then why are you letting her go out with me?'

'I don't *let* Helen do anything,' Tom retorted. 'She's not chained to me at the hip. I'm her husband, not her jailer, and I trust her. It's you I don't trust.'

'But—'

'I know very well what you've been up to,' Tom declared, his eyes blazing. 'You've been hitting on her, haven't you, turning on your charm, sweet-talking her? Well, you can forget it. You can take her out to dinner tonight, but that's all you're going to do. She's not on offer.'

Mark smiled. 'Certain about that, are you? Well, let me tell you something—'

He didn't get the chance to. All of Tom's resolve to keep his temper vanished and he grabbed Mark by the lapels of his white coat and slammed him up against the staffroom wall.

'Helen is *my* wife,' he thundered, rage making his voice shake. '*Mine*, do you understand?'

'And what if she doesn't want you any more?' Mark managed to gasp. 'Face it, Tom, you've been damned lucky to have held onto her this long. What have you got to offer a gorgeous woman like Helen? More years in this crummy little hospital, the occasional two-week holiday in some two-star hotel if she's lucky. It's not much of a life, is it?'

'At least I love her,' Tom exclaimed. 'At least I'm not offering her a cheap, sordid affair before I move on to my next conquest.'

'Neither am I. In fact, strange as it might seem—and, believe me, there's nobody more surprised than I am— I've fallen in love with her.'

'You wouldn't know the meaning of the word,' Tom said with disgust. 'This is just another game to you.'

'No, it's not. Believe me, Tom, I've never been more serious in my life.'

He wasn't lying. Tom wanted him to be—he desperately wanted him to be—but as he stared into Mark's handsome face he knew that he wasn't, and his grip on him loosened.

'I don't care if you've fallen in love with Helen,' he said uncertainly. 'She's mine. She loves me.'

Mark smoothed down the crumpled lapels of his white coat and walked over to the sink. 'Does she? Are you sure about that?'

No, I'm not, Tom thought, feeling a pain so deep inside him that it was all he could do not to cry out loud.

'I won't…' He shook his head blindly. 'Even if Helen doesn't love me any more…I'll never give her a divorce.'

Mark looked at him pityingly. 'People don't bother about divorce nowadays, Tom, or marriage, come to that. People do what they want, go where their heart calls them.'

'If…' Dear God, just to get the words out was agony. 'If she leaves me, the children will stay with me.'

'I don't think there's a court in the land that would agree to that,' Mark said. 'Helen's their mother. Wherever she goes, they'll go, too.'

Tom clasped his hands together until the knuckles showed white. 'If we weren't in a hospital—'

'You'd knock me down, punch my nose?' Mark nodded. 'Go ahead and do it if it will make you feel any better.'

Tom stared at him impotently. He wanted nothing more than to hit him, to smash him into tiny fragments, to obliterate him from the face of the earth, but Mark was right. It wouldn't solve anything. The only person who could solve anything was Helen. She had to choose between them, and what woman in her right mind would choose what he had to offer?

'I thought you were my friend,' he said with difficulty, and Mark shrugged.

'All's fair in love and war, mate.' He walked to the staffroom door and opened it. 'I'll be round at eight to collect Helen.'

Mark didn't close the door as he left, and for a moment Tom stood in the centre of the staffroom, listening to the familiar sounds of the hospital—the ping of the lift, the muffled drone of voices in the distance, the squeak of a trolley's wheels—and then he lifted Mark's empty coffee-cup and hurled it into the sink where it shattered into a dozen broken pieces.

*   *   *

'I can thoroughly recommend the steak and the lemon sole, madam,' the waiter declared as Helen stared at the menu and tried hard to concentrate.

'I don't know... I...' She shook her head indecisively. 'What are you going to have, Mark?'

'The fish, I think.'

'I'll have the same,' she declared, handing back the menu to the hovering waiter with relief.

'Liz was right,' Mark remarked, glancing round. 'It's nice here.'

And expensive, Helen thought. In fact, she could probably have fed Tom and the children for a week on what Stephano's was charging for a three-course dinner for two.

'You're worth it, Helen,' Mark said, clearly reading her mind. 'Whatever it costs, you're worth it.'

It was a nice speech, a pretty speech, but as the waiter brought Mark the wine list all she could think as she stared at the happy, chattering couples around them was, What in the world am I doing here?

She'd never intended accepting Mark's invitation, had told herself she never would, and yet here she was, wearing her best green dress, sitting in a candlelit room with a man who'd told her quite blatantly that he wanted to make love to her.

She must have been out of her mind.

No, not out of her mind, she realised, shifting her gaze to the white damask tablecloth in front of her, the glittering array of silver cutlery. Angry. Angry with Tom for saying nothing when Mark had asked her out. Angry with him for not seeming to care whether she went with him or not.

Even when Mark had arrived to collect her, Tom still hadn't said anything.

Mark had. Mark had said she looked gorgeous, and beautiful, and she'd blushed like a teenager, but Tom... Tom had stared silently at them both, his face like stone, and yet still she wished she hadn't come.

'Relax, Helen,' Mark murmured, apparently reading her mind. 'This is supposed to be a pleasant evening out for you, not the culinary equivalent of a visit to the dentist. Look, if Tom didn't like the idea of you coming out with me, he could just have told you so, couldn't he?'

'Tom doesn't tell me anything, Mark,' she said defensively. 'I make my own choices.'

'So what's the problem?'

How to explain to him—how to make him understand that she felt uncomfortable being here with him, uncomfortable at the thought of Tom left at home, looking after their children.

'Mark—'

'Did I ever tell you about the time I spent on a cattle station in Australia?'

He hadn't, but he proceeded to, and by the time they'd finished their hors d'oeuvres she was smiling. By the time they'd eaten their lemon sole she was helpless with laughter, and when their pudding arrived she was resting her chin on her hand, gazing at him, spellbound.

'You've had such an interesting and exciting life,' she said wistfully.

'A smelly one, too.' He grinned. 'Especially when I ended up in that cow manure.'

She laughed. 'Why did you leave Australia?'

He shrugged. 'I've always had itchy feet.'

'Which is why you're off to Canada on Sunday,' she said. 'I've only ever been abroad once…'

She came to a halt as she remembered why she'd gone abroad. It had been for her honeymoon. She and Tom had gone to Venice for their honeymoon, and she'd thought it was the most beautiful city in the world.

Not that she'd seen that much of it, she thought, her lips curving unconsciously. She and Tom had spent most of their time in bed, making love in the mornings, and in the afternoons, as well as at night.

'I've always wanted to travel, of course,' she continued quickly, suddenly realising that Mark was waiting for her to continue. 'India, China, America—'

'Then come with me to Canada.'

Her chin slipped off her hand with a bump. 'I...I can't.'

'Why not?'

'Because this is where I live,' she floundered. 'My home's here. My husband, my family, my work.'

He shook his head impatiently. 'Helen, when are you going to face up to the fact that all you are to Tom is a housekeeper and a mum? The spark went out of your marriage years ago, and the two of you are just going through the motions, like so many couples do. You know it, and I suspect Tom does, too, but he just can't work up the courage to tell you so.'

Was he right? She didn't want him to be right, but...

'Tom loves me,' she said, and Mark shook his head again.

'If he loved you he wouldn't have let you come out with me tonight.'

'Mark, he trusts me.'

'He just doesn't care.' He reached out and trapped her hand in his. 'Helen, I can give you so much more than Tom ever has. Oh, I know my track record with women is lousy,' he continued as she tried to interrupt, 'but I can change. If you come with me to Canada, I will change.'

'Mark, what you're suggesting...' It was crazy, mad. 'I can't just walk away from my marriage. What about my children?'

'They'd come with us, of course.'

'You want my children, too?' she said, stunned.

'Helen, they're a part of you,' he said gently. 'A very important part. Of course I want them.'

'Mark...' It was all going too fast, everything was moving far too fast, like being on a runaway train without any brakes, and one of them had to be sensible. 'Mark, you're asking me to throw away my marriage on the strength of an attraction. You don't know me—not really—and I don't know you.'

'I know I've fallen in love with you. I know I've never felt this way about anyone before. What else is there to know?'

He made it sound so easy, so simple, but it was anything but that.

'Mark—'

'I'm not asking for an answer tonight,' he said. 'That would be unreasonable, putting too much pressure on you, but...' He gently cupped her cheek in his hand. 'Will you at least promise to think about it? To think about what we could have?'

She managed to nod. There wasn't anything else she could do, not with his green eyes holding hers, refusing to let her look away.

They drove home in silence. To her relief he didn't suggest coming in for coffee, but when she started to get out of the car he stayed her for a moment and feathered a kiss across her lips.

'Just remember that I love you, Helen Brooke,' he murmured, his face serious under the streetlight. 'Whatever decision you come to, don't ever forget that.'

She was too confused to reply. She simply got out of the car, watched him drive away, then went into the house, praying that Tom might have gone to bed. But he hadn't.

He was stretched out on the sofa in the sitting room, an unopened book on his lap, and he looked as though he'd been there since she'd left.

'Are the children in bed?' she asked unnecessarily.

'They went up over an hour ago.' He cleared his throat. 'Did...did you have a good evening?'

The words sounded as though they'd been wrenched out of him, and she glanced across at him quickly, then away again.

'It was a lovely meal. Were the children OK?' she continued. 'No problems with their dinner or getting them to bed?'

'No.'

'It's going to be a beautiful day tomorrow,' she ploughed on to fill the silence. 'There's not a cloud in the sky, just a million stars and a huge moon.'

'Sounds romantic.'

Oh, Lord. She hadn't meant to make it sound so, but she was finding his steady gaze unnerving.

'Would you like a coffee—or tea—or something?' she asked.

'No. Thank you.'

Was that all he was going to say? OK, so she supposed—tried to tell herself—that she should be flattered that he obviously didn't intend grilling her about her evening with Mark, but she didn't feel flattered. In fact, as she stared down at him all she was aware of was an overwhelming desire to throw her shoes at him one by one, then tip him off the sofa, but she didn't.

'I'm tired,' she said instead. 'I think I'll go up to bed.'

He nodded, but he didn't say anything—didn't trust himself to say anything.

He wanted to. He wanted to leap off the sofa, drag her into his arms, and yell, 'You're *my* wife, God damn it, *mine!*'

He'd wanted to do the same thing when she'd left with Mark for Stephano's. Wanted to tell her how lovely she looked, her cheeks flushed with faint colour, her eyes large and bright. Wanted to beg her not to go, to stay home, but if he'd done that he would have been admitting he didn't trust her, and he could never let her think that.

But that didn't mean he was simply going to roll over and allow Mark to take Helen away from him, and if Mark thought that then he didn't know him.

And he didn't, he realised as he listened to the sounds

of Helen moving about upstairs, getting ready for bed. Back in med school, poaching his girlfriends had been par for the course to Mark, but Helen wasn't his girlfriend, she was his wife, and he was going to fight Mark with everything he could think of.

He'd spent the last two hours working it out. He'd have to make a few phone calls, take a trip into town, and it might take a few days to organise, but once the arrangements were made…

'All's fair in love and war, mate,' Mark had said.

'Too damn right it is, mate,' Tom muttered grimly. 'Too damn right.'

CHAPTER NINE

'IF THERE'S such a thing as reincarnation, I'm definitely coming back as a man next time,' Jennifer declared as Helen wrapped the blood-pressure cuff round her arm. 'No PMS, no stretch marks, no varicose veins or droopy boobs, and when I get old everyone will say how distinguished I look instead of, "Who's that wrinkled old bat?"'

Helen chuckled as she stared at the blood-pressure gauge. 'Sounds good to me.'

'How's my blood pressure this morning?' Jennifer asked, seeing her frown.

'Perfect, actually,' Helen murmured. 'And your pulse, heart rate and urine sample are fine, too.'

'You sound disappointed,' Jennifer said with a nervous laugh, and Helen smiled.

'Puzzled would be more accurate.'

And she was puzzled. Just eleven days ago Tom had been sufficiently worried to ask Jennifer to come back to have her blood pressure checked again. He'd even written 'Possible pre-eclampsia developing?' on her notes, and yet today Jennifer's blood pressure was completely normal.

'How do you feel in yourself, Jennifer?' she asked. 'No problems with your ankles swelling, no breathlessness or pain in your chest?'

'I'm feeling fine, Doctor, honestly I am,' the woman insisted. 'In fact, the only thing that's bothering me is having to go to the loo a lot more often than I did before.'

Helen unwrapped the cuff and shook her head. 'It looks to me as though you might just be one of those women whose blood pressure fluctuates when you're pregnant.'

'Is that good or bad?'

'Annoying would be more accurate,' Helen replied her brown eyes twinkling. 'We doctors don't like the unexplained. It gets us twitchy. OK, I'll make you another appointment to see me in a month's time, but I can't guarantee you'll actually see me. Our new consultant will have arrived by then, you see, and he'll probably want to take a look at you as you're one of our infertility patients.'

'The new consultant. He's Mr Caldwell's brother-in-law, isn't he?'

Helen's lips curved as she made a note of the date of Jennifer's next appointment in her diary. The speed with which news travelled through the hospital never ceased to amaze her. She'd only been told yesterday that Annie's brother had been appointed consultant in charge of their new infertility clinic and yet already the news had filtered down to the patients.

'I was rather hoping you'd be looking after me for the rest of my pregnancy, Doctor,' Jennifer continued, doubt and not a little uncertainty plain on her face.

'I honestly don't know what's going to happen,' Helen admitted. 'All I can say is if you *do* become one of Mr Hart's patients, he's coming to us with the very best of references, and I'm sure you couldn't be in a pair of better or safer hands.'

'I suppose so, but...' Jennifer sighed. 'I guess I just don't like change, Dr Helen.'

Nobody did, Helen thought as she showed Jennifer out, but in many ways it could be a good thing, forcing people to reassess their lives, encouraging them to sit down and think about what they really wanted from life.

As Mark had done on Tuesday night.

Canada.

Even now, three days later, she still couldn't quite believe that he'd actually asked her to go to Canada with him. He'd meant it, too, but nobody just upped sticks and moved to another country. You thought about it for weeks, months. You weighed up the pros and cons. You didn't just *go*.

You did if you were in love with somebody, her heart pointed out. If you were in love with Mark, you'd willingly go to the ends of the earth with him. *If* you were in love with him.

'Helen, have you got a minute?'

She whirled round to see her husband standing in the doorway of her consulting room, and her heart skipped a beat. 'Of course I've got a minute. What's the problem?'

'There's a patient in my room I'd like a second opinion on.'

A patient. He wanted to talk to her about a patient. She'd thought—hoped—that perhaps he might want to talk about themselves, but he didn't.

'What do you think is wrong with her?' she forced herself to ask.

'I think she may have PUPPPs.'

The girl did, and it was the worse case of pruritic urticarial papules and plaques of pregnancy Helen had seen outside a medical book.

'Why on earth didn't her GP send her to us before?' she demanded once the girl had gone. 'She said the rash first appeared when she was thirty-seven weeks pregnant, and her son's over five weeks old now.'

'To be fair to her GP, he could have thought it was a sweat rash—'

'A sweat rash that's all over her arms and back and legs, and which has blistered like third-degree burns?' Helen shook her head. 'Frankly, I don't know how she's coped. Not being able to wear anything but pyjamas for the last three months. Not being able to sleep, or breastfeed her baby, or take a shower because of the pain. She must have been climbing the wall.'

'The trouble is, GPs are so overworked nowadays,' Tom observed, getting to his feet and piling the files of the patients he'd seen that morning into his out-tray. 'Four minutes is all they're supposed to give to each patient, and even if he realised it was PUPPPs he probably thought it would disappear after she had her baby. It often does.'

'Well, it quite patently hasn't in this case,' Helen retorted. 'He should have sent her to us right away, Tom. We could have started her on steroids, but now it's going to take weeks—if not months—to cure.'

'I know.'

Of course he did, Helen thought as he sat down again. Just as he'd also not needed a second opinion. OK, so PUPPPs might be extremely rare, but Tom had considerably more medical experience than she did and he hadn't needed to come looking for her.

'You didn't really need a second opinion, did you?' she said, and saw a dull flush of betraying colour creep up his neck.

'No, I didn't,' he admitted, 'but I did want to talk to you, and it's so hard to talk at home what with the kids always about.'

'Sounds ominous,' she said, managing a smile, but he, she noticed, didn't. In fact, he looked nervous and uncomfortable, and her heart plummeted to the pit of her stomach. Well, she was the one who'd said they needed to talk, so she could hardly cut and run now, much as she might want to. 'What…?' She moistened her lips. 'What did you want to talk to me about?'

Tom lifted the letter-opener on his desk and began turning it round in his fingers. 'Do you remember the little *pensione* we stayed in for our honeymoon?'

She stared at him blankly. 'The *pensione*? Of course I remember it. It was off St Mark's Square, and we had a really stunning view from our bedroom window over one of the canals. The owner was a Mr…Mr…'

'Mr Angelis,' he finished for her, putting the letter-opener back down on his desk. 'He thought he could have been an opera singer—'

'But in reality he was actually tone deaf.' She nodded. 'I remember, but—'

'And do you remember the day I took you out on one of the gondolas because you said it would be romantic, and the wind changed, and you were horribly sick?'

Of course she remembered. She remembered every detail of their honeymoon, but why was he talking about it now, why was he reminiscing about it now?

'Tom—'

'We always said we'd go back there one day, didn't we?' he continued. 'To actually see Venice—the buildings, the churches, and museums—instead of just the inside of our bedroom.'

'I expect we will, when the children are older.'

'You'd like to go back?'

There was suddenly an arrested look on his face, and Helen gazed at him, bewildered.

'Of course I'd like to go back. Venice is a beautiful city.' But right now I don't want to talk about it, she thought. I just want you to tell me what's on your mind. 'Tom…' She swallowed and started again. 'Tom, you're obviously trying to tell me something, so why don't you just say it?'

There. She'd got the words out at last and, oh, Lord, he'd reached for that damn letter-opener again.

'Helen… Helen, we've been married for ten years, and they've been good years, haven't they? I mean, I know we've had our ups and downs recently—what couple hasn't? But on the whole they've been good years, haven't they?'

She felt cold and sick inside. *Been*. As in the past. As in it's all over, Helen.

'What are you trying to tell me, Tom?' she said with difficulty.

'That I—'

'Oh, thank goodness you're still here, Dr Brooke.' Doris beamed as she bustled into the consulting room. 'I'm afraid I've just had Admin on the phone, wondering where your E47 forms are. The ones about patient throughput?' she added as he gazed at her in confusion. 'They were due in yesterday, and you haven't sent yours up yet.'

'Does it have to be now, Doris?' he demanded. 'Couldn't it—?'

'Wait?' She shook her head. 'I'm afraid they're getting a little bit impatient. Apparently every other specialist registrar has sent up their forms apart from you, so—'

'OK, OK,' he exclaimed, striding across to his filing cabinet and yanking out a drawer. 'They're in here somewhere...someplace...'

'It's a gorgeous day, isn't it, Dr Helen?' the secretary said as Tom flicked impatiently through his files, then with a huff of annoyance started again, more slowly. 'Pity we haven't had many more like it for Dr Lorimer, especially as he's leaving us on Sunday. The poor man must think it never does anything but rain in Scotland.'

The woman's eyes were on her, thoughtful, speculative, and Helen managed to smile.

'I don't suppose Dr Lorimer came here for the weather, Doris.'

'Indeed—indeed,' the secretary said. 'He's off to Canada now, isn't he? I wonder which part? I have relatives there, and—'

'My E47 forms, Doris,' Tom interrupted, holding them out to her.

She took them from him, and glanced through them with a slowness that set Helen's teeth on edge.

'Well, they seem to be in order,' she said at last, all too obviously deeply disappointed. 'Thank goodness Dr Lorimer managed to fill in his forms correctly. It would have been the devil's own job trying to contact him once he's gone to Canada. We're going to miss him, aren't we? A regular breath of fresh air he's been, and so handsome and charming.'

'Quite,' Tom said tightly. 'Now, if you'll—'

'You'll miss him particularly, of course, Dr Helen,' Doris continued, her eyes suddenly fixed on her.

'I don't know about the "particularly",' Helen replied, cursing the colour she could feel rising in her cheeks. The colour she knew Doris was undoubtedly filing away as potential gossip material. 'But he's certainly been a great help to us, with Dr Dunwoody being away on compassionate leave.'

'Yes, but you and Dr Lorimer seem to have become such good friends while he's been here,' the receptionist said, her eyes never leaving Helen's for a second. 'Such *very* good friends.'

What did she know? Helen wondered uneasily. There was no way she could know about Mark asking her to go to Canada with him, or have seen him kiss her, but she obviously knew—or suspected—something.

'Dr Lorimer is a very easy man to get along with,' she replied, wishing the woman would just go, leave, and Tom must have thought the same because he strode over to the door and opened it pointedly.

'If there's nothing else, Doris?'

The secretary didn't want to leave. It was quite obvious that she didn't, but with the door open, and Tom standing beside it, there was nothing she could do but take the hint.

'You were right about that woman,' Tom exclaimed when Doris had finally gone. 'She's trouble.'

'And you've only just realised it?' Helen protested with a shaky laugh. 'Honestly, Tom, sometimes I think you go around with your eyes shut.'

'So it seems,' he murmured.

She glanced up at him quickly. There was pain in his eyes. A wealth of pain and heartache that she'd never seen before. Yes, she had. She'd seen it the day the twins were born, when she'd been holding onto his hand for dear life as each contraction had torn through her, and she'd never wanted to see it again.

'Tom—'

'Helen, what I wanted to talk to you about...' He bit his lip. 'We've been drifting apart recently, haven't we? I know our work hasn't helped—the lousy shifts we do—'

'Things will be better now we've got our own infertility clinic,' she said brightly, too brightly. 'We'll be able to have a lot more free time, and didn't you say that you thought David was going to be a real asset to the department, and that you'd enjoy working with him?'

'He certainly seems very able. Full of new ideas and plans, of course, but none of them sound too unrealistic or extreme.' He met her gaze. 'But that's not the point, is it?'

It wasn't. All the new staff in the world weren't going to make any difference to them if the love between them was gone. Well, she'd said she couldn't stand any more uncertainty, and doubt. She'd said she wanted to know if her marriage was over, and she took an unsteady breath.

'So...so what is the point, Tom?' she said.

'Do you...do you remember when you asked me if I'd ever been attracted to anybody else?'

Her stomach clenched into a hard knot of pain. I was talking about my attraction to Mark, she wanted to cry. I didn't ever think—suspect—that you might have fallen in love with somebody else. But you have, haven't you? That's what you're trying to tell me, and I don't want to hear it but I know I must.

'Yes. Yes, I remember,' she whispered.

'Helen...' He reached out and clasped her hand in his. The hand that bore her wedding ring. 'You've always been the most precious thing in my life, but—'

His phone jangled into life and with a muttered oath he

snatched it up, and barked 'Dr Brooke' into the receiver, and her heart sank as she watched his expression change.

'You've got to go,' she said when he slammed it down again.

It wasn't a question, but he answered it anyway.

'Liz says Mrs Lennox is still being sick after her op, and she'd like me to take a look at her. I'm sorry, Helen.'

'It's OK,' she said with a slightly crooked smile. 'I understand.'

And she did understand, but never had she resented her job so much. Never had she so wished she were a teacher, or a solicitor—anything but a doctor—as she did when Tom strode out of his consulting room.

She wanted to ask him who he'd fallen in love with. She wanted to know if it was somebody at the hospital, somebody she knew, and she wanted to know how long it had been going on.

A ragged sob broke from her, and she gripped her hands together tightly. Don't fall apart. Not here. Not when anyone could walk in. You've got to get through this day. Somehow you've got to get through this day and then you can cry, but not now, not here.

Blindly she stumbled out into the corridor, and almost cannoned into Doris.

'I'm sorry,' she gasped, trying to sidestep the woman without success.

'Are you all right, Dr Helen? You're looking very flushed.'

'I'm fine—fine,' Helen muttered, beginning to walk on, only to see Doris come after her. 'If you'll excuse me...'

'Dr Brooke doesn't look very well either.'

He didn't. In fact, he looked grey, and drawn, but there was no way she wanted to talk about Tom.

'I'm sorry, but I really do have to go,' she said quickly. 'I've a morning round to do, and—'

'I'm sure when Dr Lorimer leaves everything will be all right again, Doctor.'

What did the woman *know*, Helen wondered, coming to a halt in the middle of the corridor. She couldn't know anything, she *couldn't*.

'I don't know what you mean,' she said stiffly, and saw Doris smile. A knowing, ingratiating smile.

'Dr Lorimer's attentions towards you... Well, they've been quite marked, haven't they? And a less secure person than Dr Brooke... I'm not surprised if he's become a little jealous.'

'I can assure you that my husband hasn't had any cause to feel jealous,' Helen retorted, all too conscious that the heat she could feel sweeping across her cheeks must be totally belying her words.

'Oh, of course not,' Doris protested. 'Please, don't think I'm implying—suggesting—that you might have welcomed his attentions. Good heavens, I would never suggest such a thing, but you know how people talk.'

Especially meddlesome, gossipmongering old biddies like you, Helen longed to reply, but she didn't.

Somehow she managed to keep her temper. Somehow she managed even to smile tightly at the woman before striding towards the ward but as she walked along Doris's words kept reverberating round and round in her head.

Tom jealous? He couldn't be jealous. Tom never noticed anything. Good grief, even when it had been obvious to the entire hospital that Gideon and Annie had fallen in love, he'd been the last person to see it.

So why are you wishing that he *was* jealous? her mind demanded. Why do you care so much if Tom has found somebody else? He's been taking you for granted for years, using you as an unpaid housekeeper. Face it, he doesn't even know you're around, so why should you care what he does?

Because he's the father of my children, and Emma and John will be devastated if he leaves.

And is that the only reason you're upset? her heart asked as she opened the door of the Obs and Gynae ward.

She didn't know. She was so confused and upset, she didn't know anything any more except that she wanted to go home and stay there. But she couldn't, not when Annie was already hurrying towards her, interest and curiosity plain on her face.

'Liz just told me that Tom had a case of PUPPPs in his clinic this morning. I wish he'd called me. I've never seen an example except in medical books.'

'Believe me, it's not something you'd wish on your worst enemy,' Helen replied with an effort, noticing Tom emerging through the curtains round Mrs Lennox's bed. 'The poor woman was in agony, and all because her idiot GP didn't pick up on what was wrong with her.'

'Makes you wonder if it's wise for any woman to get pregnant, doesn't it?' the junior doctor said. 'I mean, it's bad enough knowing you're going to have morning sickness, an aching back and varicose veins and piles to look forward to, but to have a dreadful rash as well...' She shook her head. 'It's a wonder anybody ever decides to have a baby.'

Helen couldn't help but smile. 'Thankfully PUPPPs is very rare so if you and Gideon are thinking of adding to your family I wouldn't worry too much about it.' A tinge of faint colour appeared on Annie's cheeks, and Helen's eyes flew to hers. 'Annie, you're not—I mean, you and Gideon aren't...?'

'I'm not sure,' Annie confessed, her colour deepening. 'I haven't done a test yet, but I seem to have suddenly gone right off tea, and the last time I felt like that was when I was expecting Jamie.'

'Oh, Annie, I'm so pleased,' Helen exclaimed. 'Are you pleased if you're pregnant?'

'To be honest, I don't really know how I feel,' Annie sighed. 'Gideon and I talked about having children before we got married, of course, but I was sort of thinking in maybe in a year or two.'

'Our two were unexpected, and we never regretted having them,' Helen said, 'and, believe me, if you *are* pregnant, Gideon will be over the moon.'

Actually, he looked as though he could do with some good news right now, she thought. Whatever Tom was telling him was obviously going down as well as a plague of midges in a nudist colony.

'Ready to start the morning round, Helen?'

'Hmm?' she murmured, her eyes still fixed curiously on her husband.

'Patients, Helen. Remember them? Sick people in beds who need our attention?'

She turned to see Mark smiling at her, and flushed slightly.

'Sorry. I was miles away.' Quickly she straightened her white coat and affixed a smile to her lips. 'OK. Ready whenever you are.'

'*Are you out of your mind?*' Gideon asked, then swiftly urged Tom up to the top of the ward away from the prying ears of Mrs Foster. 'You're asking if you and Helen can take a week off work, starting *tomorrow?*'

'I know it's short notice—'

'It's also impossible. Mark's leaving us on Sunday, and we're not expecting Rachel back for another fortnight.'

'It's important, Gideon. You know I wouldn't ask if it wasn't.'

The consultant sighed. 'I'm sure you wouldn't but, like I said, it's impossible. Now, I can certainly give you and Helen a week off at the beginning of July—'

'Gideon, if you don't give me this week off, I'm just going to take it.'

His boss's jaw dropped. 'Do you realise what you're saying?'

Tom nodded grimly. 'That if I walk out of the hospital tomorrow without your consent I'm effectively throwing my job away. Like I said, this is important. I want to take Helen to Venice, and I've bought the plane tickets.'

Gideon stared at him in amazement. 'You're prepared to throw away your career for the sake of a *holiday?*'

'For this holiday, yes.'

Gideon glanced down the ward to where Helen was deep in conversation with Mark. 'Does Helen know what you're doing?'

Tom's jaw clenched as he followed the direction of his boss's gaze. 'No, she doesn't, and I don't want her to know. At least not yet.'

'I see. Or rather, I don't, not at all. Look, would you at least consider changing the booking—waiting until Rachel gets back?'

'It has to be this Saturday, Gideon.'

'But why?' the consultant protested. 'Why does it have to be so soon? What difference will a few days make?'

'All the difference in the world to me,' Tom said tightly.

'Yes, but *why?* What possible…?' Gideon came to a sudden halt as Mark suddenly laughed at something Helen must have said, and his eyes narrowed. 'You mean, you think that she…that she and…'

'Gideon—'

'Don't tell me any more—you don't have to tell me any more,' he said quickly. 'OK. I'll speak to Admin—tell them we need emergency cover for a week, starting tomorrow. They're not going to like it but, hey, what's new? And I expect we'll survive somehow.'

A wave of relief spread across Tom's face and he reached out and clasped the consultant's hand firmly in his. 'I owe you one for this, Gideon.'

'Too damned right you do,' the consultant said, nodding, 'and, believe me I'll collect.'

'You can put me on permanent nights when I get back if you want,' Tom replied.

'I might just do that. Now, get yourself out of here and along to Theatre before I change my mind. Oh, and, Tom…' His eyes were kind as Tom half turned and stared back at him questioningly. 'Look, I just want to say…well, good luck, that's all.'

I'm going to need it, Tom thought. Taking Helen back to where they'd spent their honeymoon was the biggest gamble of his life. Everybody said you should never go back, never try to recapture the past, but that was exactly what he was hoping to do. Hoping that if he took Helen back to the small *pensione* off St Mark's Square he might just be able to rekindle the love she'd felt for him ten years ago.

It had to work. He had to believe it would work because without Helen… Without her he would be nothing.

He glanced across at her as he left the ward. She looked puzzled and curious—probably wondering what the hell he and Gideon had been talking about. He managed a small smile, and saw her lips curve a little uncertainly in response. He couldn't imagine a world without Helen. Didn't want to imagine a world without Helen. If he could just get her away from Mark, away from his sweet-talking and his charm, maybe he might stand a chance.

He had to. Somehow he had to.

'If you're in agreement?'

'In agreement with what?' Helen floundered, dragging her gaze away from her fast-disappearing husband and back to Mark.

'You're miles away, aren't you?' He laughed. 'Mrs Merrick. I've just said I think you should start her radiotherapy next week.'

'Oh. Right. Fine.' She nodded.

'It's just that I'll be gone by then—'

'And you want to make sure all the loose ends are tied up before you go. I do understand, Mark.'

'It's not just Mrs Merrick's treatment I want tied up, you know.'

His green eyes were holding hers, and uncomfortably she glanced over her shoulder, hoping no one had heard him. 'Mark, you said you wouldn't pressurise me.'

'But this is Friday, Helen, and I'm leaving on Sunday,' he protested. 'What's there to think about? You know your marriage is over. You know I love you, and you love me.'

Did she? she wondered as he strode on to the next patient, looking angrier than she'd ever seen him. She knew she was attracted to him, but was that the same as love?

When she'd met Tom for the first time she'd been sitting in the Belfield canteen, all nervous and self-conscious in her brand-new junior doctor's white coat, when a deep male voice had suddenly said, 'Is it all right if I join you?'

And she'd looked up to see a man with dark brown hair and gentle grey eyes carrying a tray piled with food, and had thought he looked nice. He'd sat down and started talking, telling her he was a new junior doctor, too, and within half an hour she'd known that this was the man she wanted to spend the rest of her life with.

With Mark it had been so very different. With Mark she'd thought, Wow, before he'd even opened his mouth, but was that love or mere physical attraction?

Does it matter? her mind asked. If Tom's leaving you, do you really want to stay on at the Belfield, having to face the sympathetic looks, the curious questions? Wouldn't it be better to leave, to start a new life in Canada?

It sounded sensible. It sounded eminently sensible, so why could she feel tears welling in her eyes at the thought?

Never had a day seemed so endless. Never had it been

so hard for her to focus, to concentrate on what she was doing.

Yvonne Merrick was very tolerant after she carefully explained all about the radiotherapy, then couldn't remember which day Mark had said it would start. Mrs Foster wasn't nearly so tolerant when Helen dropped her file, sending the woman's notes scattering all over the place.

'It seems to me that some people need to pull themselves together,' she'd said loudly after Helen had gathered up the notes, red-cheeked with embarrassment.

'Talk about the pot calling the kettle black,' Annie commented as she accompanied Helen down the ward. 'She's hardly the most together person, is she?'

'Perhaps not,' Helen sighed, 'but I really shouldn't have dropped her notes.'

'Look, why don't you get off home?' Annie suggested. 'You've only got another ten minutes of your shift left, and I'll cover for you.'

'Are you sure?' Helen said hesitantly. 'It doesn't seem fair to run out on you, leaving you with my work.'

'Hey, what can happen in ten minutes?' the junior doctor protested, and Helen groaned as she saw Liz hurrying down the ward towards them.

'Famous last words, Annie. OK, Liz, tell me the worst. We've got a massive influx of emergencies coming in, right? And I can wave goodbye to any hope of getting off home early.'

'It isn't that,' the sister replied. 'It's…'

'It's what?' Helen asked, wondering why Liz's normally cheery face should look so white, shocked.

'It's… Helen, there's no easy way to say this. It's Emma.'

'Emma,' Helen repeated blankly. Emma was with her school's swimming team. It was competing against another school in the first round of the Glasgow Challenge Shield and she'd waved her off on the school bus this morning.

But as she continued to gaze at Liz, saw the pity and sympathy in her face, fear clutched at her heart. A horrible gut-wrenching, desperate fear. 'What's happened—what's wrong?'

'She's been hit by a car. She was crossing the road with her schoolfriends when a car came round the corner—'

'Where is she?' Helen demanded.

'In A and E. They brought her in half an hour ago, and one of the nurses recognised the name. I...I'm afraid it doesn't look good.'

Dear God, no, Helen thought as she began to run towards the ward door. Not Emma. Not her daughter. Not her bickering, complaining, lovely daughter. If she...

Desperately she shook her head. She mustn't even think the words—she mustn't. She had to get to A and E. If she could just get to A and E everything would be all right, and then suddenly Mark was beside her, his face as white as she knew her own must be.

'Helen, I've just heard. Oh, God, Helen, I'm sorry—so sorry.'

He was holding her hands, chafing them between his own, and dimly she realised he was still speaking. Murmuring the stock phrases she'd used all too often herself to relatives in emergency situations. How Emma was in the best possible place, how skilled the surgeons were in A and E. His words washed over her, empty, meaningless, trivial.

'Mark, I have to go,' she exclaimed, cutting him off in mid-flow.

'I'll come down to A and E with you, Helen. Stay with you.'

She shook her head. 'No.'

'You can't go there on your own,' he protested. 'Let me come with you, please.'

She pulled her hands free from his, and stared up into his handsome face, her eyes full of fear, and pain, and desperation, and shook her head again.

'Tom. I want…I want Tom.'

CHAPTER TEN

'WHY won't they let us see her, Tom?' Helen cried, her voice harsh, unsteady, as she paced the corridor outside A and E. 'What are they doing in there, what's taking so long?'

'They'll be carrying out tests, performing procedures...'

'But can't they at least let us see her?' she exclaimed. 'I just...I only want to see her.'

Quickly he went to her, wrapping her in his arms, trying to give her comfort, to draw some comfort for himself in return. 'She'll be all right, Helen, I know she will...'

'But how did it happen?' she said raggedly into his chest. 'Why wasn't one of the teachers keeping an eye on her?'

'They can't watch children all the time, and you know what Emma's like. She'd be so excited she'd forget all about road safety.'

'Even more reason for somebody to watch out for her. If Emma...' Her voice broke and his grip on her tightened. 'Oh, God, Tom, I feel so *useless*. I want to be in there, doing something. I want to be treating her, helping her, and I can't...I can't.'

He knew what she meant. All his years of training, all his medical experience, and yet now—when it really mattered, when it was their own child's life that was at stake—he was standing outside in a corridor, useless.

'She'll be all right,' he repeated with more confidence than he felt. 'She's spunky, strong—'

He came to a halt as the door to A and E clattered open. The consultant was walking towards them, and there was a smear of blood on his white shirt. Emma's blood, Tom

realised, and desperately he fought against the wave of
nausea that threatened to engulf him.

'How…how is she?' he said, his voice seeming to sound
from somewhere far away.

'I'm afraid she's one very ill little girl. Her pelvis is
shattered, and her left lung has collapsed. The pelvis will
mend in time, as will her lung, but we ran a CT scan
because of the injury to her head, and…'

And?' Tom said with difficulty.

'She has an extradural haemorrhage. We need to perform an immediate craniotomy to relieve the pressure on
her brain.'

Tom's eyes flew to Helen's. An extradural haemorrhage.
The artery running over the surface of the outer layer of
Emma's brain had ruptured, and blood was seeping into
her brain. The only way to stop it was to drill holes into
Emma's head and then try to clip the ruptured blood ves-
sel. Sometimes the procedure worked, but sometimes…

'Can we see her?' Helen said, her voice shaky, uneven.

The consultant was already walking back towards A and
E. 'Only for a minute before we take her to Theatre. Now,
please try not to be too upset by what you see. She's connected to a battery of tubes and wires—'

'We're doctors,' Helen said quickly. 'We know what to
expect.'

'In theory you do,' the consultant observed, 'but this is
your daughter, and that makes it a whole different ball
game.'

He was right.

Helen had thought herself hardened—toughened—after
so many years of working with ill and often dying patients,
but as she gazed down at her daughter she knew nothing
could have prepared her for this.

It wasn't just the wires and tubes connected to the various monitors, or the endotracheal tube in Emma's throat,
helping her to breathe, that tore at her heart. It was the

sight of her daughter's little face swollen beyond recognition, the livid red marks on her fragile body where she'd been dragged along the road by the car.

'Tom… Oh, Tom…' She squeezed her eyes shut, trying to contain her tears, but they leaked past, trickling down her cheeks, running into her mouth, and he put his arm round her.

'She'll be all right—she's strong—she'll be all right,' he said, his jaw working rapidly, his own voice clogged.

'I'm afraid that's all the time we can give you,' the consultant murmured, beckoning to his waiting staff.

'Just one more minute—a second,' Tom begged, then leant forward and gently kissed his daughter's forehead. 'We're here, sweetheart. Mummy and I are here, and everything's going to be all right.'

Emma didn't move, didn't even open her eyes, and desperately Helen reached for her daughter's hand.

'Emma, it's Mummy. We're going to make you better. I promise—I *promise*—we're going to make you better.'

'We really do have to go,' the consultant insisted.

They had time only to nod, and then the trolley was moving. Out of A and E, along the corridor, the IV bags swinging, the respirator wheezing, and they had to run to keep up with it, Helen holding one of Emma's hands, Tom the other, knowing they were getting in the way, but they had to be there. Just had to.

'I'm sorry, but you can't come any further,' one of the nurses said when they reached the theatre. 'Look, why don't you go through to our waiting room?' she added more gently, seeing their faces. 'There's tea, and coffee-making facilities, and someone will come and speak to you as soon as there's any news.'

'How long will it be before we know anything?' Tom asked.

'I don't know. I'm sorry, but I honestly don't know,' the nurse replied. And then Emma was gone, the swing doors closed and Helen pressed her hand hard against her lips, trying to hold onto the feel of Emma's small fingers in hers.

'Helen…?'

There was pain in Tom's grey eyes, a pain she knew was mirrored in her own, and blindly she followed him into the small room marked PRIVATE. They 'had a similar room in Obs and Gynae, and it was a room she'd always hated. The room where they gave relatives bad news. A room of heartbreak and tears.

She drew in a shuddering breath, and then a new panic assailed her as her eyes fell on the clock on the wall. 'Tom, it's after five. School will be over. John—'

'Annie's gone to collect him. She said she'd look after him for as long as it takes.'

'Oh, that was kind of her,' she said tremulously. 'So kind.'

And necessary, she realised as they sat in the waiting room and the minutes dragged slowly by. Minutes that became hours, until her nerves were paper thin. Just when she thought she'd go mad if they didn't get some news soon the consultant appeared, looking exhausted and drained.

'OK, the good news is we've relieved the pressure on her brain and repaired her pelvis and lung,' he declared. 'She's on her way to Intensive Care now, and…'

'The bad news?' Helen faltered, knowing from his face that there was definitely bad news.

He sat down, forcing them to do the same. 'You have to remember that the human brain was never designed to withstand the impact of a car. When the car hit her she was dragged along the road for quite some distance—'

'What are you saying?' Helen interrupted. 'What are you trying to tell us?'

'That she could be brain damaged,' Tom murmured, his

face chalk white. 'You're trying to tell us she might be brain damaged, aren't you?'

The consultant nodded. 'I'm afraid there's a distinct possibility of that, yes.'

Helen let out a low moan of pain, and Tom gripped her hand quickly.

'And when...' He cleared his throat, and when he spoke again his voice sounded rusty, unused. 'When will we know for certain?'

'Not until she regains consciousness. In cases like this, the quicker she does the better the prognosis tends to be, but for the moment I'm afraid all we can do is wait.'

'Can we go up to Intensive Care—see her?' Helen whispered.

'Of course, but then I would suggest you go home, get some sleep. It's after midnight—'

'I'm staying,' Helen said firmly.

'I really don't think—'

'I'm staying, too,' Tom interrupted, and the consultant smiled a little ruefully.

'I thought you might. I'm afraid we can't offer you much in the way of accommodation—just somewhere to sleep and wash—but, please, use it. You won't help your daughter by getting ill yourselves.'

'Is there anything we can do to help Emma?' Helen asked as they followed the consultant along the corridor and up the stairs to Intensive Care.

'Talk to her. It doesn't matter what the subject is—the weather, the price of beans. The brain's a funny thing, and even though you might think she can't hear you, there's very strong evidence to suggest that the sound of your voice could bring her back.'

Bring her back? Did the consultant mean Emma might slip into a coma? People could stay in a coma for weeks, months. There were cases of people staying in one for years.

Helen glanced quickly across at Tom, and he met her gaze.

'Do you remember when she was three and she fell off her tricycle and hit her head on the pavement? And then when she was five, she ate some of your birth-control pills?'

An uneven chuckle broke from her. 'She...she does seem to be accident-prone, doesn't she? But—'

'She got through all those crises,' he declared, 'and she'll get through this one, too. We'll get her through it, Helen. We will.'

We.

Never had the word sounded so good. Never had she so needed to hear it. He might have fallen in love with somebody else but he wasn't going to abandon her, leave her to go through this alone. And she couldn't go through it alone. As they walked into the intensive care unit, and she saw the array of all too frighteningly familiar monitors, and Emma lying so waxen, so still, with only the slow rising and falling of her little chest indicating that she was still alive, Helen knew that she could never have gone through this alone.

'I know everything looks a bit scary,' a plump nurse said understandingly as she checked the IV bag hanging over Emma's head. 'But everything's there for a purpose. I'm Sue, by the way,' she added. 'Sister Kate and I will be looking after your daughter while she's with us so if you want or need anything, just let us know, OK?'

I just want her back, Helen thought as the nurse bustled away. I want my Emma back, being loud and snippy, and fighting with her brother, and being a right royal pain. I just want her *back*.

'She's strong,' Tom said firmly, clearly reading her mind. 'She'll come through this. I know she will.'

Where did Tom get his certainty, his strength? She wished she had half of it. Talk to Emma, the consultant had said, but how could she talk when all she wanted was to rage and scream at the unfairness of it, and then burst into tears?

'It doesn't matter what we talk about, remember,' he said. 'All we have to do is talk—let her know we're here.'

'I know, but…'

'It's OK, Helen, it's OK,' he murmured, and he lifted their daughter's hand and began to talk.

He talked to Emma about her schoolfriends, her favourite CDs and the holiday they'd spent in Cornwall last year. He talked through the long dark night and into the next day until his voice was cracked and hoarse, his face grey with fatigue, and as Helen sat beside him and listened she wondered why in the world she had ever been attracted to Mark Lorimer.

What she felt for him wasn't real. It was a fantasy, created because she'd felt neglected, taken for granted, and when Mark had paid attention to her, flattered her, she'd thought it was love. It wasn't love. It was what you felt for a film star you fantasised about, or an actor on TV, but Tom…. Tom was real, and honest, and she loved him.

And now he'd found somebody else. Somebody he loved more than her. But she wasn't going to give him up without a fight. Not Tom. Not her Tom.

Saturday passed in an endless blur of cups of coffee, of sandwiches eaten but not tasted. Emma was taken off the ventilator to see if she could breathe on her own, and to their relief she did, but still she didn't move or open her eyes.

'You really should try to get some sleep,' Sue said, gazing critically at them both when she came on duty. 'If you're not careful, the pair of you are going to end up ill, and that won't help Emma at all.'

'I'm fine,' Helen insisted, and Tom nodded his agreement, but the nurse shook her head.

'Far be it for me to call a specialist registrar and an SHO liars, but neither of you look particularly fine.'

She was right, they didn't, but how to explain to the nurse her feeling that if she fell asleep Emma might lose her grip on life and die?

'I'm fine,' she repeated, and Sue sighed but she didn't press the matter.

'Do you want anything to eat?' Tom asked once the nurse had moved to the bottom of the unit to talk to one of her colleagues. 'A sandwich—some soup?'

Was it morning or night—breakfast or lunchtime? It was impossible to tell in the windowless surroundings of Intensive Care.

'Just a coffee, please,' she replied.

'I won't be long,' he said, and as he left she knew he wouldn't be.

He hadn't left her side, apart from essential things like going to the toilet or getting her something to eat or drink. Always he'd been there, bolstering her up, telling her to be positive. But it was so hard to be positive.

If Emma died…

Stop it, she told herself, closing her eyes tightly to stop the hot tears she could feel welling in her eyes from trickling down her cheeks. Falling apart isn't going to help anybody, least of all Emma. Tom says she can hear you, that she's going to get better, and you've got to believe that, because if you don't it means you've given up hope, and you mustn't ever do that.

'Mummy, why are you crying?'

Helen's eyes flew open. Had she imagined it? Surely she must have imagined it, but as she glanced down a cry came from her—a cry of joy, and relief, and overwhelming thanks. Emma's eyes were open and she was looking at her.

'Emma…. You…you know me?'

The girl frowned. 'Of course I do. What kind of dumb question is that?'

The best dumb question in the world, Helen thought, beckoning frantically to Sue who ran towards her, took one look at Emma, then shot out of Intensive Care to find the consultant.

'Mummy, you didn't answer me,' Emma continued. 'Why are you crying?'

'Because…' Helen gave a hiccuping laugh. 'Because I'm so happy, sweetheart.'

Emma's frown deepened. 'That's even dumber. Nobody cries when they're happy.'

'It's a mum thing.' Helen smiled through her tears. 'When you're older—have children of your own—you'll understand.'

'Where's Dad?'

'I'm here, love.'

He was, and Emma shook her head and sighed when she saw he was crying, too.

'Don't tell me. It's a dad thing, too.'

Tom could only nod, and when the consultant arrived and performed various tests, they waited on tenterhooks until he pronounced himself well pleased.

'She's turned the corner at last, but I think this young lady needs to rest right now,' he said with a smile, seeing Emma's eyelids beginning to droop.

'She's going to be all right?' Helen said anxiously. 'I mean—'

'She's not going to lapse into unconsciousness again,' the consultant reassured her. 'She's going to be just fine, Helen.'

And she wanted to kiss him, but she knew she probably shouldn't so she reached for Tom instead, and he hugged her, and she sobbed into his neck with relief and joy.

'Oh, Tom, I thought… I was so frightened that…'

'I know, I know,' Tom said, his cheeks as wet as hers. 'But she's all right, Helen. She's *all right*.'

'You must go and tell Gideon and Annie,' she declared. 'They've been so good to us—covering for us so we could stay here, looking after John.'

Actually, they'd been marvellous. When Helen had tried to thank them, Gideon had got cross, and Annie had shrugged off her thanks impatiently.

'You'd have done the same for us if we'd needed it,' was all she'd said.

'Are you sure you'll be OK if I go up to Obs and Gynae?' Tom asked. 'I don't like to leave you.'

Her heart contracted slightly. She wished he meant that, but there would be time enough to talk about their marriage later.

'I'll be fine,' she said with an uneven smile. 'I might try to get some sleep. You go up to the ward, and give Annie and Gideon the good news.'

'Mr Hart will be pleased to hear it, too,' Sue declared, overhearing her. 'He popped in earlier this morning to ask how Emma was.'

'David Hart's here?' Tom exclaimed, and the nurse nodded.

'He said he had an appointment with your boss to discuss your new infertility clinic.'

'Then today's…?'

'Sunday.'

An odd expression had appeared on her husband's face and Helen gazed at him with concern. 'Tom, are you OK?'

For a second he didn't answer, then he straightened his shoulders. 'I won't be long, Helen.'

'Take as long as you like,' she declared. 'Like you said, everything's all right now.'

And it was, she thought, tenderly staring down at her daughter as Tom hurried away. Emma was sleeping, but it was a natural sleep now, not that awful, terrifying, unconscious one.

'It's time you got some sleep, too,' Sue said firmly, and Helen laughed shakily.

'Do I look that bad?'

'Actually, you look like one very relieved mum.'

I feel like one, too, Helen thought as she left Intensive Care, but Mark clearly didn't think so as he came round the corner and saw her. He took one look at her tear-stained face, and strode towards her, his hands outstretched. 'Oh, Helen, I'm sorry, so sorry…'

'No, no, you've misunderstood,' she cried. 'She's just woken up, Mark, and she knows us. Emma *knows* us.'

He stared at her in disbelief, then whirled her around in his arms.

'Oh, Helen, that's wonderful news—the very best. I was coming to say goodbye. I'm just leaving for the airport, you see, and—'

'You're leaving right now?' she interrupted.

'You can't have forgotten that this is my last day.' He laughed, but in truth she had.

In truth, she hadn't thought about him at all since Emma had been taken to Intensive Care.

'Mark—'

'I've been trying, and trying, to persuade the authorities at my new hospital in Canada to let me stay on here for another month, but they've point-blank refused to budge, and I've been wondering how I was going to give you my support when I'm in Canada, and you're here in Glasgow, but now…' He smiled. 'Everything's going to be fine.'

Tom would never have gone to Canada and left her alone with Emma, she thought as she stared up into Mark's handsome face. Tom wouldn't have suggested that somehow, some way, he might manage to give her long-distance support, and Tom wasn't even in love with her any more.

She held out her hand to him. 'Good luck in Canada, Mark. I hope it turns out the way you want.'

'But you'll be able to find out yourself,' he exclaimed. 'When you join me there.'

'Join you there?' she echoed. 'Mark—'

'When Emma had her accident I bought you an open plane ticket, which means you can fly out to Canada to join me whenever she's fit enough to travel.'

'Mark, I'm not going to Canada.'

'Not for a while, of course,' he agreed. 'Emma will probably be in hospital for quite a while yet, then she'll need physiotherapy—'

'Not ever, Mark.'

The smile on his face faded. 'But I don't understand. I thought it was all arranged, agreed, between us.'

'I'm sorry, Mark,' she said gently, 'but I'm staying here. I have to.'

'But why?' he protested, his green eyes puzzled, confused. 'Your marriage to Tom is over—'

'Not if I can save it, it's not.'

'You *want* to save it?' he exclaimed. 'But why? I love you, and you love me…' His lips twisted as she gazed up at him awkwardly. 'You're trying to tell me you don't love me, aren't you?'

She didn't want to hurt him, but neither could she let him go on believing something that wasn't true. 'Mark, what I feel for you, and what I feel for Tom… It's not the same, and it won't ever be.'

'You're saying you still love Tom?' he gasped, and when she nodded he shook his head. 'But, Helen, I could give you so much…'

'Maybe you could, but it's not the same as giving me what I want, is it?' He didn't understand. She could see that he didn't understand, and quickly she held out her hand to him, not sure whether he would take it or not, but he did. 'Take care of yourself in Canada, Mark.'

'You take care, too, and…well…' He shrugged. 'I guess all I can say is, be happy.'

'I'll try,' she replied, smiling a little tremulously, and he reached out, and gently touched her hair.

'I do love you, you know.'

'I think you might think that you do.'

'No. I don't think, I know.'

'Mark—'

'I know, I've said enough.' He straightened up with an effort. 'Look, can I ask a favour? It will take you away from the hospital for a couple of hours, so if you want to refuse I'll understand.'

'What sort of favour?' she said uncertainly.

'Will you come with me to the airport? I know it's silly,' he continued as she tried to interrupt, 'but I won't be coming back to Scotland, and I'd very much like your face to be the last one I see when I leave.'

She owed him that much, she knew she did, and she nodded. 'All right, I'll come.'

And she would. She'd go out to the airport with Mark, and then she'd come back, and somehow, some way, she would win her husband back to her.

'It's wonderful news about your daughter,' David Hart said as he accompanied Tom to the lift. 'It must be a great relief to you and your wife.'

'It is,' Tom replied. 'Emma will have to undergo physiotherapy for her pelvic injury, of course, and they'll be monitoring her lung and head injuries, but the consultant is hopeful she might be able to leave hospital in three to four weeks.'

'That's tremendous,' David Hart said. 'I don't have kids myself, but I know how I would have felt if it had been my sister Annie's boy. Please, give my very best wishes to your wife, and tell her I'm so happy everything is going so well for her and for you.'

Not everything, Tom thought with a heavy heart as he shook David's hand and stepped into the lift. Emma was going to fully recover, but he and Helen…

If Emma hadn't had her accident they would have been in Venice now, in the small *pensione* with the creaking bedstead, but now…

Take it one day at a time, Tom, he told himself. Mark is leaving today, so you can take it one day at a time. All right, so Glasgow might not be able to rival Venice in the romantic stakes, but Helen's still here with you, and you still have a chance to win her back.

But only if he could actually find her, he thought with a rueful smile when he found the small bedroom off Intensive Care empty. So much for Helen's promise to try to get some sleep. Knowing her, she was probably still sitting by Emma's bedside. But she wasn't.

'Do you know where my wife is?' he asked, as one of the junior nurses hurried past.

'She's gone, Doctor.'

'Gone?' he repeated blankly. 'Gone where?'

'To the airport with Dr Lorimer.' The girl looked at him curiously. 'Are you all right, Dr Brooke?'

'Yes,' he managed to reply. 'Yes…I…I'm fine.'

But he wasn't fine. He was anything but fine as he stumbled out of the unit.

She'd gone. Helen had gone. Without a word of farewell, without even so much as a goodbye, she'd just gone to Canada with Mark.

How could she have done that? To leave him was one thing, but to leave Emma and John?

Well, she could just go if she wanted to, he thought savagely. He wasn't going to beg and plead with her to stay. If she wanted to go with Mark then he and Emma and John would get along just fine without her.

Only they wouldn't. Without Helen… A low moan came from him as he felt his heart twist and break inside.

Without Helen he wouldn't be living, only existing. He had to change her mind, make her stay. He didn't know how he was going to do it, but before he even thought about what he was doing he was racing towards the hospital exit, praying he'd get to the airport in time.

'There's still time for you to change your mind, you know,' Mark said as he and Helen stood together at the departure gate. 'OK, so you'd be travelling without so much as a toothbrush, but we could buy everything you need in Toronto.'

Helen shook her head. 'I've made my choice, Mark.'

'You have, and I'll never understand it. OK, OK, I'll say no more,' he continued ruefully as she tried to interrupt. 'I just hope Tom realises what a very lucky man he is.'

Her smile slipped a little. 'You'd better get going or you'll miss your flight.'

'I guess so,' he murmured, then the corner of his lips twitched slightly. 'No chance of a farewell kiss, I suppose?'

'Better not,' she replied, and he grinned.

'You don't know what you're missing.'

He was wrong. She did, but she didn't want to be reminded of it. Not now. 'Goodbye, Mark, safe journey.'

He nodded and reached for his hand luggage, but as he began to walk through the departure gate a pretty girl with long black hair collided into him. 'Hey, what's your rush?' he demanded.

'Sorry,' the girl replied, clearly harassed. 'But I'm late for my flight to Toronto.'

'Now, there's a coincidence.' Mark smiled. 'I'm going there, too.'

And he would never change, Helen thought as she watched him walk off with the girl, his hand already under her elbow, his head bent to catch whatever she was saying.

Flirting was as instinctive to him as breathing, and he must have read her mind because just before he disappeared from sight he glanced over his shoulder and threw her a smile—half apologetic, half rueful—and try as she might, she couldn't stop herself from smiling back.

She hoped he would be happy in Canada. She hoped he would find what he was looking for there, but she knew where her own heart lay, and quickly she turned, intending to get a taxi back to the Belfield, only for her heart to leap into her throat as she saw Tom running towards her across the concourse.

'Tom, what's wrong? Has something happened to Emma?'

'Emma's fine,' he said breathlessly. 'It's you I've come to see. You I've come to stop.'

'To stop?' she repeated in confusion as the loudspeaker suddenly crackled into life, announcing the last call for boarders for flight 101 to Toronto. 'To stop me from doing what?'

'Going to Canada with Mark,' he said raggedly. 'Helen, don't go. Please, please, don't go. Stay with me and the kids.'

'Stay with you? Tom—'

He gripped her by the arms, and she was amazed to feel that he was trembling. 'All I want is for you to give me another chance. I know we've been having problems. I know you love Mark, and not me, but if you could just give me another chance, maybe…maybe in time you might forget him and grow to love me again.'

She stared up into his, oh, so familiar face, a face that was ravaged with fatigue and worry and pain, and tears filled her eyes. Tears of relief and joy and love. He thought she was in love with Mark. That was why he'd been so cold, so remote. Not because he was leaving her, but because he thought she was leaving him.

'Tom, Mark and I—'

'If you want to leave the Belfield—go to another hospital—then we'll go,' he said desperately. 'If you want to leave medicine completely, and raise chickens on a farm, or move to the Western Isles and become a potter, we'll do it, but, please…please, don't leave me. You are, and always will, be everything to me.'

She didn't know whether to laugh or cry, and did both.

'Tom, I'm not going to Canada. I have absolutely no intention of going to Canada.'

'You haven't?' he faltered. 'Then why…?'

'Mark asked me to come to the airport to see him off, and that's what I've just done,' she said, gesturing to the plane that was ready to taxi down the runway.

He gazed at it for a second, then back at her. 'Helen, if you're staying with me because of Emma—'

'Tom, I'm staying with you because I *love* you,' she said. 'I fell in love with you ten years ago, and I haven't ever really stopped loving you.'

'But, Mark… What about Mark?'

'I was flattered by him. Flattered that somebody so handsome and charming could be interested in me. He made me feel special, and for a little while I thought that was the same as love, but it wasn't.'

'Helen…' He swallowed hard, and his grey eyes held hers, refusing to allow her to look away. 'I don't really want to know this, but I have to ask. Have…have you and Mark made love?'

Oh, how thankful she was that she could look him in the eye and say, 'No.'

The breath went out of him quickly, but he didn't take his eyes off her. 'Did…did you want to?'

Yes, I wanted to, she thought. Wanted to because Mark made me feel like a woman again, and not just a wife and a mother. Wanted to because you seemed to be taking me for granted. But how could she tell Tom that? Tom, who'd

never stopped loving her. Tom, who'd said she was everything to him.

'I might have been flattered by his attention,' she replied, willing him to believe her, 'but, no, I didn't ever
want to make love with him.'

'And you'll stay with me?' he said, his voice rough with
emotion. 'You won't leave me?'

'Only if you ask me to raise chickens or become a potter
in the Western Isles,' she said with a shaky laugh. 'Tom,
I *hate* chickens. They've got big claws and beaks, and they
peck and flap their wings, and I couldn't make a pot to
save myself.'

'All I want is for you to be happy,' he murmured. 'Just
tell me what you want that will make you happy.'

'You make me happy,' she said softly. 'You and John
and Emma make me happy.'

'But—'

'Just love me, Tom,' she said. 'All I have ever wanted
is for you to just love me.'

He gathered her to him, and held her tight. 'Helen, I fell
in love with you the first day we met in the Belfield canteen, and I've never stopped loving you. I know I haven't
said it often enough, but I'm going to from now on.'

'We have to talk, too,' she said. 'We have to keep remembering that we're a couple, and not just doctors. We
forgot to talk, Tom, forgot what was really important in
our lives. Yes, we're doctors, but we're people first, a couple first.'

'Can we…? Do you think we can go back to the way
we were?' he asked, and she thought about it for a moment.

'I think we can be better than we were. Stronger, closer,
if that's what you want.'

'*If?*' He kissed her long and hard. 'Helen, when I'm
ninety-two, and bent, and bald, I will still love you.'

'And I will still love you, Tom,' she whispered.

'Together for always?' he murmured, and she nodded.

'Together for always, Tom.'

2 FREE

books and a surprise gift!

We would like to take this opportunity to thank you for reading this Mills & Boon® book by offering you the chance to take TWO more specially selected titles from the Medical Romance™ series absolutely FREE! We're also making this offer to introduce you to the benefits of the Reader Service™—

- ★ FREE home delivery
- ★ FREE gifts and competitions
- ★ FREE monthly Newsletter
- ★ Exclusive Reader Service discount
- ★ Books available before they're in the shops

Accepting these FREE books and gift places you under no obligation to buy, you may cancel at any time, even after receiving your free shipment. Simply complete your details below and return the entire page to the address below. *You don't even need a stamp!*

YES! Please send me 2 free Medical Romance books and a surprise gift. I understand that unless you hear from me, I will receive 4 superb new titles every month for just £2.60 each, postage and packing free. I am under no obligation to purchase any books and may cancel my subscription at any time. The free books and gift will be mine to keep in any case.

M3ZEA

Ms/Mrs/Miss/Mr ....Initials....................................
BLOCK CAPITALS PLEASE

Surname ....

Address ....

....

....Postcode................................

Send this whole page to:
UK: FREEPOST CN81, Croydon, CR9 3WZ
EIRE: PO Box 4546, Kilcock, County Kildare (stamp required)